Well, look what snuck in while I was in the kitchen.

Zach should stay away—he really should—but knew he wouldn't. Casually making his way across the room, he stopped to check in at a few tables while keeping Sadie in view. Her laughter, her smile were beautiful things, though she wasn't overtly flirting. Still, a surprising surge of anger streaked through him. He found himself circling slowly, almost like a lion studying his prey from all angles.

Coming in from behind, he could no longer see her face, but he could finally hear her words.

"So did they know someone was sabotaging the mill before this?"

Every cell in his body went alert at the question. Why was she asking?

"Oh, yeah," one of the locals eagerly replied. "Of course, those of us that work there knew it way before any manager did."

She nodded, which caused the muted lighting to glint off her ruby curls.

Standing right behind her, Zach felt a moment of evil satisfaction that he stood so close, yet she seemed unaware. Every time he was around this woman, his hackles rose.

He wasn't sure whether to shake her or kiss her.

* * *

Expecting His Secret Heir is part of the series Mill Town Millionaires from Dani Wade.

Dear Reader,

My mama used to say that when you married someone, you married their family, too. In *Expecting His Secret Heir*, family is the one thing that brings Zach and Sadie together—and the very thing that keeps them apart. Family can be complicated, happy, troubled or, in this case...a secret.

Zach and Sadie are each working hard to keep their families safe, and I was amazed how such noble intentions could cause so much conflict between two people trying to do their best. Still, they can't stay away from each other. Will they both get what they want? Or will one of them have to sacrifice their good intentions on the altar of a new family waiting in the wings?

I'd love to know what you think about Zach and Sadie's story! You can email me at readdaniwade@gmail.com or keep in touch with me through my website www.daniwade.com. I'm also active on Facebook at www.Facebook.com/dani.wade.1.

Enjoy!

Dani

DANI WADE

——

EXPECTING HIS SECRET HEIR

Recycling programs
for this product may
not exist in your area.

ISBN-13: 978-0-373-73482-5

Expecting His Secret Heir

Copyright © 2016 by Katherine Worsham

Printed in U.S.A.

HARLEQUIN®
www.Harlequin.com

Dani Wade astonished her local librarians as a teenager when she carried home ten books every week—and actually read them all. Now she writes her own characters, who clamor for attention in the midst of the chaos that is her life. Residing in the Southern United States with a husband, two kids, two dogs and one grumpy cat, she stays busy until she can closet herself away with her characters once more.

Books by Dani Wade

Harlequin Desire

His by Design

Mill Town Millionaires

A Bride's Tangled Vows
The Blackstone Heir
The Renegade Returns
Expecting His Secret Heir

Visit her Author Profile page at Harlequin.com, or daniwade.com, for more titles.

To the Worshams, Tates, Nelsons, Schafers and Raymos, for teaching me all that family can mean during the highs and lows of life.

One

From her crouching vantage point, Sadie Adams sized up the composition before her with an artistic eye.

Wide, straight shoulders of a towering man, silhouetted against the smoking buildings and rubble. A small strip of dead cotton plants in the foreground. The sun lightening the top of his thick head of hair, leaving the rest of him in shadow. Standing in profile, hands on his hips, head hung as if in despair.

As the shutter clicked, she wondered about his story. Had he been an employee of the ruined mill behind him, or was he there to help? As several men approached, he raised his head, giving her a clearer view of his rough-cut features.

I should have known.

Those broad shoulders, clothes that fit a tight, strong body in all the right places—he was the most capable man she'd ever known. The most incredible lover she'd ever had. The one it had almost killed her to walk away from.

Zachary Gatlin was the reason she was back in Black Hills, South Carolina. But he could never know that.

She took a few more pictures, surreptitiously inching in the other direction, as he talked with the men surrounding him. Yet she kept Zachary Gatlin in her line of sight. Five years ago, he had blended in with the crowd. A worker bee. Now, he was clearly in charge, directing those around him with decisive gestures and a firm tone that reached her even though she couldn't make out the words.

Had he worked his way up into management at the mill? Would that change how he treated her? Would it change how he saw her?

Moving along the edge of the parking lot, she attempted to get closer to the ruined buildings. Her high-quality camera had some amazing close-up capabilities that she was eager to test. The piece of equipment was a luxury she couldn't afford—but her employer could, and he was pulling out all the stops to ensure she got the information he needed. She should feel dirty for accepting the camera, but it was the one thing—the only thing—she didn't regret in her current situation.

If Zachary knew the truth, he'd make sure she deeply regretted ever coming back here. He wouldn't rage or get physical. He wouldn't need to. That dark stare and hard features would be enough to make his point. At least, that was the Zachary she'd known—or thought she'd known.

Would he be the same now?

Turning to the smoking ruins, she focused on the things she knew. Angle, lighting, depth, perception. Her circumstances had prevented her from pursuing photography at a professional level, even though she'd had a few photographs published, thanks to a friend. But if her life had been different, with fewer obligations, maybe she could have followed her own dreams instead of lying awake at night wondering how her family would all survive.

Lost in her art, she'd almost blocked out her surroundings until a masculine voice spoke near her. "Ma'am?"

For just a moment, her heart jump-started. Had Zach finally spotted her? But she turned to find a generic security guard by her side. "Yes?"

"If you'll come with me, please?"

Though it was a question, his firm gesture in the direction he wanted her to go brooked no arguments.

After ten steps she had no doubt where he was leading her. Desperate to delay the inevitable, she paused. "Excuse me? Could you explain what happened here?"

Possibly fooled by her innocent expression, the

man stopped, too, and cocked his head to the side. "You aren't from around here, are you?"

She shook her head. "No. I've visited before, and really wanted to come back. But I didn't think I would find the quiet place I remembered in such an uproar."

That was the truth. The single hotel in the area had been booked full. Sadie had managed to get the last room in the last B and B with an opening. From the types of people she saw coming and going, most of the influx consisted of firefighters and construction crews. From the looks of the half-full parking lot, quite a few of those guys were out here today.

"I kinda guessed, based on the accent," he said with a smile.

Yep. No matter how she tried to tame it, her Texas breeding colored her every word.

The guard went on, "Well, the admin building on this side of the plant had a bomb go off in it."

Sadie made herself look surprised, even though she'd picked up this tidbit of information around town already. "Really? Who would want to do that? This is the main source of employment for the town, if I remember right."

"It sure is," the man said, shaking his head. "They say they have a suspect in custody but haven't released any names yet." He stared up at the building for a moment, looking confused. "I have no idea why someone would want to ruin the mill, but after all the bad stuff that's happened around here in the last year—"

"Steve," Zach barked from over a dozen feet away.

"Oops. Better get movin'," the guard said.

Each step felt like a final walk down death row, but Sadie forced herself to move. After all, making contact with Zach was the reason she was here. She needed to spend as much time with him as possible—and she hoped their previous one-night stand might give her a bit of an in, even if the fact that she'd disappeared after it wouldn't make it a positive in.

Zach still had a group of workers around him who parted as she drew near. She expected them to skedaddle now that the boss had new business, but no. Not a single one moved away.

Her petite five-foot-five stature had been the bane of her existence ever since she'd realized she wouldn't be growing anymore, and being surrounded by a bunch of six-foot-tall men did not set her at ease. She felt like David approaching Goliath against his will.

Not that she had any sort of righteousness on her side.

There was only a moment to study Zach up close. His thick jet hair was a little longer than it had been the last time she'd seen him. Remembering that night long ago, she couldn't help the itch to bury her fingers in those silky strands again. Or to run her fingertips over the weary lines of his chiseled features until the tension melted away.

Her sensual memories were dimmed by the current hard look on his face. There was no glimmer of recognition or softening as she stood before him, even though she could remember every detail of the body that now towered over her. No smile of welcome softened his sculpted lips as he asked, "What are you doing?"

"I'm just taking some pictures," she said quietly, lifting the camera still in her hand.

If anything, his dark eyes hardened more. "On private property."

She glanced around, uncomfortable under the stares of the other men. "This is…was a business, right? There aren't any signs posted about private property or trespassing."

"That's because they were all blown down by the bomb."

Really? She wanted to challenge him, push past that stony facade to find out if he was simply making that up. Was he trying to punish her for walking away? Or did he really not recognize her? Had she been that unmemorable? The thought made her slightly ill.

She settled for a simple, "Sorry, I didn't realize."

Zach stared her down. What would he do next? She had a feeling this wasn't going to end as a friendly little chat. Her cheeks started to burn. Inwardly cursing her fair skin, she tilted her chin up to counteract the feeling of inadequacy. So what if he didn't remember her…she'd still find a way to get what she needed.

But she couldn't force her gaze back up to his.

"As you can see, this is still an active fire zone, and we've got a great deal to investigate before we know how safe it is."

She smirked at the lame excuse. "I wasn't anywhere near the fire. I was in the parking lot with a bunch of other people."

The crowd around her shifted, as if uncomfortable with her spark of courage. But Zach didn't back down. "Do you have a press pass?"

"What?"

"A press pass," he said, enunciating each word with careful control. "Do you have permission to be taking photos of the scene?"

She seriously wanted to roll her eyes at his show of dominance but held herself in check. "No."

"Steve, please escort this lady back to her car."

Startled, she snapped her gaze up to meet his eyes once more. Surely he wasn't throwing her off the property?

He stepped closer, close enough for her to catch the scent she'd missed all too often, mixed with perspiration from his work despite the cool October air. His fingers—the same ones that had explored her body that long-ago night—caught her chin, tilting it up just a touch more until it was uncomfortable. Then she had no choice but to meet his gaze, despite their height difference. Her heart thumped hard, though she didn't know if it was from his nearness or fear.

"I suggest you stay away from where you don't belong."

As the guard escorted her back to her car, she had only one thought.

Guess he does remember me after all...

Zach Gatlin stood behind his desk, lost in thought as he stared at the large monitor. Where had she come from? Did he really want to know?

Unfortunately, he did.

As much as he wished he could forget the red-haired beauty he'd taken to bed five years ago, the memory of her eager passion had resurfaced all too often. As had the memory of her love of sunsets and people and nature—her artistic eye had taught him to see the gentler world he'd forgotten in the midst of war.

Then, with no warning, she was gone. He'd consoled himself with the thought that if she hadn't been willing to say goodbye, she wouldn't have stayed in the long run anyway. Probably for the better, since Zach's responsibilities were a heavy load.

Sometimes he wondered if that inner voice lied.

Shaking off the memories, Zach focused on the present. The question was: Did he look into her or not? Running a background check would be all too easy, especially now that he ran his very own security business. The tools were within close reach.

Close enough to make his fingers twitch. He could know all he wanted within minutes, every small detail of her life within days.

But was it the right thing to do?

Maybe he should have asked himself that before he threw her off mill property yesterday. He'd had a gut reaction to seeing her there, so close but seemingly oblivious to him. He wished he had controlled himself, but what was done was done. He couldn't go back.

With his life, he knew that all too well.

Turning away from the computer, he decided to confront this problem head-on rather than hide behind snooping. Security might be his business, but it didn't have to be his life.

Thirty minutes later, he wondered if he should have taken the easy way out. Figuring out where Sadie was staying had been easy—this was, after all, a small town. Getting past the nosy owner of the B and B? Well, that was an altogether different problem.

"Gladys, I know she's here, I just need to know what room she's in."

"Is she expecting you?"

"Probably." At least that much was the truth. If Sadie remembered anything at all about him, it should be that he was a man of action.

Gladys leaned against the high desk in the foyer. "Now, why would Black Hills's newest hero want to see some strange woman who just came into town?"

Lord, this woman wanted a pound of flesh, didn't she? "I haven't always lived here, Gladys."

"So you met her somewhere else?" Was that a gleam of excitement in her eyes? How sad that his life had gone from daily drudgery to full-on gossip mill fodder.

He'd met Sadie right here in Black Hills, but it had seemed like another time and place. "The room number?"

Probably recognizing the obstinate look on his face and realizing she wasn't getting any gossip from him— outside of his very presence here—Gladys relented. "Room three."

Back straight, he refused to look over his shoulder to see her watching him as he climbed the stairs. He hesitated before knocking, but luckily there was no one to see it.

The door opened, revealing Sadie. She was just as he remembered her, with smooth, translucent skin, an abundance of fiery red hair and green eyes that appeared guileless. A trap he wasn't falling for this time.

"Zachary," she said.

He stalked through the doorway. The suite was more spacious than the tiny hotel room she'd occupied the last time she'd been here. This was open and airy, with a lightly feminine touch. His gaze bounced away from the bed in an alcove and came to rest on the laptop in a low sitting area in front of a fireplace. He made his way forward with measured steps.

"It's been a while, Sadie," he finally said.

"Five years," she murmured.

He paused, giving away the fact that he'd heard her when he would have preferred not to show any reaction at all. He was ashamed to admit, even to himself, that he'd often thought about what he would say if he ever saw her again. He'd pictured himself as calm, slightly condescending as he asked her why she'd left without a word, without any explanation.

Nothing in that scenario came close to the amped-up emotions he was experiencing at the moment.

Eager for a distraction, he paused in front of the open laptop. Several pictures shared space on the screen, showcasing the smoldering mill from different angles. He'd never had much time for art, but to his inexperienced eyes, these looked pretty good.

Which for some reason made him even angrier.

"You weren't authorized to take pictures there."

"Did you tell that to every bystander in that parking lot with their cell phones in their hands? Or just me?"

He glanced in her direction, mildly surprised by her return salvo. He hadn't known her to be very confrontational. Not that they'd spent much time arguing, but they had talked—a lot. He wouldn't have called her a doormat, exactly, but she'd shown a lot more spirit in the last twenty-four hours than he'd seen in the week he'd known her five years ago. A week that had ended in a night he couldn't forget.

She raised one fine brow. "There were no signs posted. No one said I couldn't be there...at first."

He studied the images a bit longer. Damn if she didn't have him stumped. What exactly had he wanted to accomplish by coming here? To go over the same territory as at the mill? To find out why she had returned? To get information without having to ask any direct questions?

To put himself out there to be hurt again?

Gesturing toward the screen, he asked, "So you came back just for pictures?"

It was as close as he'd let himself get to addressing the elephant in the room. He really wanted to know why she hadn't come back for him. She was the one woman he'd ever felt he could actually let into his life, have a real relationship with. And she'd walked away without looking back.

"I was in the area and heard about the explosion. I wanted to check it out."

She looked too calm, acted too casual. And she just happened to be in the area? He shook his head. When had he gotten so suspicious?

"What about you?" she surprised him by asking. "What were you doing there?"

That's when he realized she wasn't the only one who had changed in five years. "I'm head of security for the Blackstones—"

She smiled. "Wow. That's really great. Going from maintenance to head of security is a big jump."

He knew he shouldn't, but he said it anyway. "I'm

not head of security for the mill. I handle security details for the entire family and all of their interests. I run my own security firm." Bragging did not come easily to him. Not that he'd ever had much to brag about. But somehow it felt good to rub his success in Sadie's face.

He wasn't the same man she'd met then—recently returned from combat in the Middle East, fighting the nightmares while maintaining a strong facade for the women in his family he'd spent a lifetime supporting.

Then one night he'd let her in, and he wished she'd never seen that side of him.

"Until we can get a good look inside and evaluate the damage, the mill is a huge security risk. So the Blackstones have asked me to oversee this initial part of the investigation."

"I heard it was a bomb."

He nodded. Yep. A bomb set off by a crazy man.

"Any suspects?"

It was a natural question. Simple curiosity. So why did his muscles tense when she asked?

"Yes, but that information is not being released to the public."

The words came out in a more formal tone than he would have normally used, but it was all for the best. Keeping their distance meant keeping himself sane. Instead of leaning in to see if her hair smelled the same as it did before.

He did not need to know that.

He eyed the bright waves dancing around her shoulders. He definitely didn't need to know.

"So it would be better to stay away from there right now." *And away from me, so all these emotions will respond to my control.* "Wait until we can guarantee it's safe."

"In the parking lot?"

"Right." He didn't care if she wasn't buying it. A man had to do…

Suddenly realizing he'd accomplished nothing but torturing himself during this visit, he stalked back to the door. Unfortunately, she followed, until she was within arm's reach. He was too far away from the door to escape.

It all flooded back—all the memories he'd struggled to hold at bay since that first moment he'd seen her again at the mill. The way his heart pounded when she laughed. The way her soft voice soothed his nerves as she told him a story. The way his body rose to meet the demands of hers.

So many things he couldn't force himself to forget.

But he could force himself to walk away this time. "I'll be seeing you, Sadie," he said, as casually as he could.

She pulled the door open and smiled. "Definitely."

Something about her tone, that confident edge, ruffled him, pushed him to throw her off balance. He couldn't stop himself. He stopped in front of her, bending in low to place his mouth near her ear. He sucked in a deep breath. "So…" he said, letting the word stretch, "aren't you gonna tell me why you really left?"

Her gasp left him satisfied…for now.

Two

Sadie's entire body instantly snapped to attention. She might not have moved, but every nerve ending was now awake and focused on the man before her.

She hadn't thought he'd directly address her leaving. Indeed, he'd seemed to do everything but ask the all-important question: Why? She'd thought she was prepared. Her flippant answer rattled around in her brain for a moment, but she couldn't force it out.

Instead she stared up into his brooding dark eyes and lost her breath. She'd known she would hurt him, leaving like that. He'd never tell her so, but she couldn't help but wonder if it were true from his somber gaze.

His body seemed to sway a little closer, and her

mouth watered at the thought of his lips on hers once more. Then the trill of her phone broke the moment of silence.

Suddenly he was back to arm's length, leaving her to wonder if she'd imagined that moment. Wished it into being.

His eyes grew wider, reminding her that her phone was still ringing. She ignored both him and the phone. Her mother called late in the evening, when her duties for the day were done. Only one person would be calling her at this time of day, and she wasn't about to speak to him in front of Zach.

Her heart pounded. She licked her lips, trying to think of something to say.

Instead of waiting for an answer, Zach gave a quick smirk and then walked out the door without another word. She waited until he was down the stairs and out of sight before pushing the door closed. Then she dissolved against it like melting sugar.

Tears welled, along with the wish that things didn't have to be this way. She quickly brushed both away. Her life had been one long lesson in dealing with reality, not dreaming of fairy tales.

At least he hadn't forgotten her.

Forcing herself to her feet, she crossed to the sitting area and picked her phone up off the low table. The very name she expected flashed across the screen. She sucked in a deep, bracing breath, then touched the screen to call him back.

"I'm listening."

She hated when he answered the phone like that. The part of her that rebelled against what she had to do forced her to hold her words just a minute longer than necessary, garnering some petty satisfaction from making him wait.

"What do you need, Victor?" she asked.

"Ah, Adams. Where were you?"

The impersonal use of her last name grated on her nerves, but she was, after all, simply a servant. "Away from my phone."

"Don't get uppity with me, Adams. Just because you're hundreds of miles away from Texas doesn't mean you're off the leash."

Right. Remind her of the dog she was—that would make her work harder. But it was an apt description—she was a hunting dog. Sent to search for and fetch exactly what her owner wanted.

"I apologize," she said, hoping he couldn't tell her teeth were gritted. "But I didn't think you wanted me to answer the phone and give you an update in front of Zachary."

"Very good, Adams. I knew I could trust your judgment."

As if it had been all his idea. If Victor Beddingfield had an original idea ever in his life, she'd be shocked. Of course, this little expedition was his idea—and here she was. But the idea wasn't original to him. His father had tried it first.

"So you've already made contact? Good girl."

Yep, she was definitely a dog to him. "I have, but he's not happy about it."

"You simply have to make him like it. You know how to do that…don't you?"

She wished to goodness Victor had never found out the truth about her last visit to Black Hills. Not that he cared about her choice to deceive his father, telling him that Zachary couldn't possibly be the son he sought. The longer Zach had been out of his life, the more of their father's money Victor could spend. Still, the knowledge had given him a weapon to use against her—but not the biggest one.

"This might take some time." Although, even if she had all the time in the world, Zach would probably never forgive her—then or now.

"Well, we don't have time, remember?" he said, his voice deepening in a way she perceived as a threat. "I need money. Now. And I'm sure you do, too—or rather, your sister does."

Not really. Amber didn't worry about that sort of thing. The hospital treated her cancer, that was all she knew. It was all Sadie wanted her sister to know. The practical aspect—bills, scheduling, medical decisions—all of that was handled by Sadie. Some days, it was enough to make her feel like she was drowning, but she did it anyway. It kept her sister alive, for now. It allowed her mother to be at her sister's side for however much longer they had her. That was all that mattered. Still, the reminder struck home.

But Victor wasn't done. "So get me the dirt I need to disinherit him, and we will all be in a much better position. Got it?"

How could she not? "I understand. I'll do my best."

"Good girl."

One of these days, Sadie's teeth were going to be worn to a nub, just from the irritation of listening to this guy. "He's not giving me much to work with," she said, consciously relaxing her jaw.

"Then get creative," Victor said. Without another word, he disconnected the call.

Get creative.

Sadie sighed. Easy for him to say. Victor had always had someone to do the dirty work for him. Her role in his father's household made her a convenient option. Her role in his father's investigation of his older son five years ago told Victor she wasn't just convenient, but experienced.

Now he wanted the investigation into Zach reopened so he could discredit the man who didn't know he was Victor's older brother.

Time for Sadie to earn her keep.

Plopping down onto the couch, she stared at her computer screen. Get creative. How? She couldn't think of any way to get around Zach's present uncooperative state. She needed to get close to him, learn everything she could about him. But he wanted her nowhere near him.

Glancing around to remind herself that she was alone, Sadie clicked on the computer folder she'd closed when Zachary had knocked. Instantly the screen filled with images of him. There were pictures from all different angles, taken while he wasn't looking. Not for Victor's benefit. Not because she had to. Because she wanted to.

Because the single photo she had of him from her last visit wasn't nearly enough to last her a lifetime.

She hadn't dared take home any more, certain that her employer, Victor and Zach's father, would discover them and realize she was lying about how much she'd found out about Zach.

She studied the haunting image she'd gotten of Zach silhouetted against the smoking building from yesterday. The contrast of his strength with the ruins of the mill reminded her of his conscientious care for his family, his quiet way of watching those around him until he saw a need that he could fill. If only he could fulfill her needs, free her from this mess of a life so she could be with him once more.

No, she couldn't think like that. This was her problem to solve, as always. If Zachary knew what she was involved in, he'd lead the mob running her out of town. The town didn't know her, either. They'd protect their own.

At least, that was the perception she had from watching him at the mill. But did she really know? What could the town tell her about Zach that he wouldn't tell her himself?

She studied the picture once more. She needed to

find out, and she had an idea how she might make that happen.

I need more information.

And she wasn't going to get it moping in her room. Grabbing a light jacket against the autumn chill, Sadie threw a quick glance at the computer to make sure it was off, then headed out the door.

She shouldn't worry about her laptop. But Victor had taught her that people did all kinds of things that served their own ends—and invaded other's privacy. She never wanted to be caught off guard again.

Not that she had many secrets, but Victor had managed to find a doozy.

She paused on the stairs. Zach had said he owned a security firm now. Would he have checked her out?

Even now, had he figured out who she was? How long after that would he find out who her employer was, and what he meant to Zach?

Once that happened, her mission would be over before it even began. The ticking time bomb had been set.

Luckily, the overly friendly proprietress of the bed-and-breakfast was at the front desk when Sadie reached the office. The woman's husband was as reticent as she was open, so he wouldn't have been nearly as helpful. For now, luck was with Sadie.

The woman even started the conversation in the direction Sadie wanted it to go.

"Wow! New to town and already getting visits from the local hero."

Technically it was a statement, but Sadie could hear the question beneath the words. And Gladys wasn't finished. "Of course, not everyone feels that way…"

Interesting.

"Why is that?" Sadie didn't feel the need to beat around the bush. Subtlety wasn't Gladys's forte.

"Oh, there was a big to-do when he came home. He graduated to officer in the military, survived combat. Then came home to take care of his family after his mama's heart attack."

Sadie murmured a few encouraging words, even though Gladys didn't need them.

"But then all those plants got poisoned earlier this year—"

That made Sadie's ears perk up. "What plants?"

"Cotton fields." The older woman leaned toward Sadie over the high desk in what Sadie had learned was Gladys's favorite position. "One of the things Zach did to earn money was crop dust. Early this spring he dusted nigh on half the county in a day. By morning, the plants were dead. Boy, did that cause an uproar."

"I bet." Probably more like a riot. Killing the cash crop of choice for the area… "Did the police get involved?"

"You bet. Quite a spectacle it was, though I wasn't there. Handcuffs and all. But they released him the same day."

Gladys lowered her voice, though they were the

only two around. "Them Blackstone brothers got involved. And they obviously believe in him, because he's the biggest news story around here...besides the bomb, of course."

"You mean his new job?"

The woman nodded, her tight gray curls bouncing. "He don't have to work three jobs now, that's for sure. I hear his business is taking off like hot cakes."

See, he doesn't need the money.

Sadie pushed away the seductive thought. She wouldn't sugarcoat what she was doing. Regardless of his current circumstances, Zach deserved the inheritance her late boss had wanted to give him. The one she had denied him because she had lied and told Victor's father that Zach wasn't, in fact, the son he sought. She'd been afraid he would corrupt Zach the same way he had everything else around him.

Still believing his firstborn was out there somewhere, Beddingfield Senior had willed him his inheritance. The only way for Victor to get it was to ruin Zach. Because he knew the truth...the truth behind the lies she'd told.

Desperate times called for desperate measures.

Gladys had just given her a place to start looking for Zach's dirty laundry. And if Sadie succeeded in her mission, she'd steal away every last dime.

From Zach.

Three

"I heard there was an incident at the mill yesterday."

Of course she had. Zach glanced over at his sister. Despite her engagement to the richest man in town, KC had kept her bartending job, and she heard everything. "You mean besides the fire?"

"Well, this was a bit more interesting than a bomb, in my opinion. It was about you…and a woman."

Only KC would find that more interesting. But since there was never any gossip connecting him to any women in town, he could see her point of view.

Zachary hated that he paused before answering, practically admitting his guilt. "You heard about that?" His sister was too smart for him to bother pretending he didn't know what she was talking about.

Her sassy attitude was displayed in a raised brow and hand on her hip. "Seriously? This is a bar. In a small town. People in here have nothing to do but talk all day…" She studied him in a way that made him want to squirm. "Did you really throw her off the property?"

"You make it sound so much worse than it was."

KC's eyes widened. "Zach! Why would you do that?"

He wanted to use his lame security excuse again, but he seriously needed better lines. Instead, he focused on pulling a beer. "Let's talk about it later— we're kinda busy right now."

"That we are," KC said, filling her tray with drinks for a rowdy table of off-the-clock firefighters. The dinner hour was just approaching, and Lola's bar was already filled to capacity. "But you're not off the hook," she warned him.

He wanted to let his rare bad temper loose and tell her to mind her own business, but knew his sister's fiancé, Jacob Blackstone, wouldn't pull any punches putting him in his place if Zach made his own sister cry. Besides, it wasn't KC's fault.

It was Sadie's.

He hadn't been able to stop thinking about her, to the point that he wished his brain had an off switch. Even sleeping hadn't given him any relief. Ever since seeing her two days ago, he'd dreamed of the single night they'd been together, and the glorious sensuality of her body.

The images in his brain were not calming him right now. Any part of him...

He distracted himself by checking on his orders in the kitchen, along with the two new hires he'd put in place a month ago. One was a veteran chef from the military who'd put in ten years of duty before losing a leg in Afghanistan. The other was a hard-working kid who reminded Zach a lot of himself at his age, with a single mom and baby sister at home to support. Only Miguel's dad had been killed in a car accident. Zach's had simply walked away when supporting a wife and child got too boring for him to handle.

Despite the rush, he found everything moving along smoothly in the kitchen. There was no need for Zach to be working at Lola's. In fact, he refused to let his mother pay him anymore. The last thing he needed these days was money—a concept he couldn't quite absorb. But he couldn't stay away.

Taking care of his grandmother, mother and sister was a way of life for him. He'd only been away from them while he was in the military. No matter what his job was now, his day still wasn't complete until he'd touched base with them. And he wasn't the kind of man to sit around while the women worked. He wasn't like his father—uncaring enough to walk away from the people who needed him. Nor KC's father, who'd done the same when the going got tough. Zach had never let down the women in his life, and his new millionaire status wasn't an excuse to start now.

So here he was on a Friday night, carrying a tray of appetizers out to a table surrounded by several couples eager to eat before hitting the dance floor. Lola's was crowded tonight. Lots of people were in town needing to blow off steam, especially those who worked out at the mill. Too many probably thought about the disaster they would have faced if it hadn't been a mandatory shutdown weekend when the bomb had gone off.

Zach talked to the customers for a few minutes about the damage, then left them to their food. As head of security, he'd done his best to spread the most positive outlook. He hoped he was having some effect, because the last thing this town needed was for the people living here to give up. Regardless of the damage, the Blackstone brothers were not going to let the mill close and the town disappear. They'd all worked too hard to have that happen to the people they cared about.

Hearing some boisterous laughter, Zach glanced at the table of firefighters only to spot an unexpected redheaded beauty in their midst.

Well, look what snuck in while I was in the kitchen.

He should stay away—he really should—but knew he wouldn't. Casually making his way across the room, he stopped to check in at a few tables while keeping Sadie in view. Her laughter, her smile were beautiful things, though she wasn't overtly flirting. Still, a surprising surge of anger streaked through him. He found himself circling slowly, almost like a lion studying his prey from all angles.

Coming in from behind, he could no longer see her face, but he could finally hear her words.

"So, did they know someone was sabotaging the mill before this?"

Every cell in his body went alert at the question. Why was she asking?

"Oh, yeah," one of the locals eagerly replied. "Of course, those of us who work there knew it way before any manager did. But we needed proof, right?"

She nodded, which caused the muted lighting to glint off her ruby curls.

"They say they got someone in custody," the man continued. "Whoever it is, they're gonna get a sh— oops, not supposed to say that in front of a lady."

Was that a hint of a blush on the curve of her cheek he could actually see?

"But the whole town, they're already up in arms."

"That will just give them a target," she murmured, nodding her understanding.

Standing right behind her, Zach felt a moment of evil satisfaction that he stood so close, yet she seemed unaware. One by one the men at the table spotted him. Oddly enough, none gave away his presence to the lamb in their midst.

Every time he was around this woman, his hackles rose. He told himself it was because he'd found her at the mill, where she didn't belong, but he was afraid the reason was much, much deeper.

"Why would you want to know?" he finally asked.

Sadie jerked around to face him, causing her drink to slosh over the rim and drip from her fingers. "What are you doing there?" she asked before lifting her hand up and gently sucking the moisture away.

Zach ignored the tightening in his groin, ever aware of his surroundings and a half dozen pairs of eyes glued to their interactions…and that was just at this table. Zach gave a short nod in the direction of the men, then cupped Sadie's elbow with his palm. "Let's get you a fresh drink."

Without waiting for a response, he ushered her around a dozen tables to get to the less crowded, more utilitarian end of the bar. The whole time his heart pounded with intensity, though he wasn't sure why the conversation affected him that way. He forced himself to speak quietly. "Why are you asking all those questions?"

Sadie didn't jerk away, but she kept up a firm pressure with her arm until he let her free.

Zach ignored KC's curious glances from several feet away, grateful that there were enough customers to delay her interrogation. He turned back to his prey. "What was that all about?" he demanded again, letting anger seep through his self-control.

At first, he thought she would cave and spill her guts. His stomach churned as he realized he wanted to know everything about why she was here, why she'd walked back into his life and turned his emotions on their head.

Then her thick lashes swept up, revealing those gorgeous green eyes, and somehow he knew he wasn't getting what he wanted tonight.

She wiggled her glass. "I thought I was here for a fresh drink?"

He wasn't sure whether to shake her or kiss her, but he felt relief as he moved behind the bar. Being that close to Sadie only encouraged his circuits to misfire.

So he tried a different tactic. He let his fingers slide slowly over hers as he lifted the glass from her hand. Her lowered lashes told him she had something to hide. At least that secret he could guess, if her reaction was anything like his.

"You know those guys?" he asked as he refilled her Coke. He wanted to grin at her drink of choice. As far as he'd been able to tell, she didn't drink, smoke or get into trouble. Her innocence simply hinted at an incredible sensuality that he'd never been able to forget.

She shrugged delicate shoulders. "A couple of the guys are staying at the B and B. The hotel ran out of room."

They'd been lucky with all the crews that had come in to help fight the fire and pull debris. Unfortunately, Black Hills wasn't very well equipped for visitors. Every last vacant room was in use at the moment. There were even a couple of fire chiefs bunking out at Blackstone Manor.

"I told them there was a great place for food and

drinks out this way. They invited me to join them when I was free. I hope that was okay?"

The glance from under her lashes didn't seem to be seeking permission so much as a reaction.

It was his turn to shrug. "I've always been easy to find."

Her petite body stilled. She glanced around, as if making sure no one was close enough to listen. "Look," she said, "I'm very sorry about leaving. I just got…scared."

He stepped closer, bypassing the safety of the counter. "Why?"

She swallowed, hard. His instincts were to follow the movement with his mouth, taste what he could only see.

Reaching out, he forced her chin up with demanding fingers. "Why?"

"It was just too much for me," she whispered.

Without thought, he found himself murmuring, "Me, too."

Startled eyes met his. He could drown in all that fresh green color. Five years ago, her eyes had been just as vibrant. Just as alluring. He'd fallen for her seductive pull and received the rudest awakening in his life for it. But he still couldn't forget the night spent drowning in her green gaze.

Suddenly Sadie was bumped from behind, breaking the hold she had on Zach. Quickly he shuttered his expression.

He stepped back once, twice, until he found his

breathing distance. "Now, what's with the questions?"

"Why? Do you see me as a threat?"

In more ways than one. But he wasn't giving her more ammo, so he bit his tongue. "Should I?"

Her gaze dropped at his question, causing his hackles to rise once more. Why was getting any information from her like pulling teeth?

"Just don't stir up trouble." He turned away, lifting a tray of dirty glasses off the counter and stepping through the opening behind the bar.

Only then did he hear her say, "And how's a busy guy like you gonna stop me?"

"Don't you know you don't have to do this anymore?" a male voice from right behind Sadie asked.

Zach turned back toward her, focusing over her shoulder with a grin that she wished was directed at her. But it was better than the glower she'd been sure to receive after her challenge.

"My mama doesn't care how much money I make," Zach said. "She simply points at a table and tells me to get busy."

When Zach came back out from behind the bar she was forced to step to the side, giving her a good look at the newcomer.

Or rather, newcomers. The trio looked like the epitome of wealth…and exhaustion. Zach shook hands with the blond man before turning to do the same with a man whose dark hair had a mind of its own. The woman between them received a light, social hug.

Based on her discussions with people in town, these must be the Blackstones.

If she remembered her gossip correctly, this would be Aiden Blackstone, his wife, Christina, and one of the younger brothers, Jacob. The utter weariness in their expressions spoke to the trials of the last week. Their brother Luke was currently in the hospital after being near the epicenter of the exploding bomb.

Suddenly another woman arrived through the break in the bar counter, pushing Sadie even farther back. The blonde beauty threw her arms around the one Sadie assumed was Jacob, holding nothing back. The surrounding people didn't seem surprised. The woman pressed light, quick kisses against his lips, then settled at his side. Her touch never wavered and never dropped. If Sadie remembered correctly from local gossip, Zach's sister, KC, was engaged to Jacob.

Zach studied them a moment, then asked, "How's Luke doing?"

"Much better," Jacob said. "They say he can come home tomorrow."

"No further damage to his legs?" KC asked.

Jacob shook his head. "None."

"Good," Zach added. "We don't need any more damn tragedies around here."

Everyone murmured their agreement.

"Anyway." Aiden stepped closer. "My wife is in

firm need of sustenance that isn't hospital food, and I promised her some of your mama's fried chicken."

Zach grinned in a way that took Sadie's breath. "With a baby on the way, that woman should have anything she wants to have. She's doin' all the work, after all."

"Amen," Christina said, leaving the whole group laughing.

Sadie smiled, even though she knew it was a little sad around the edges. The group reminded her of her family. There were only three of them, but she, her mama and her sister had taken care of each other through a lifetime of heartache. They could often make each other laugh during the hardest times. And they never gave up hope that they would be together.

Zach stepped back to the kitchen to put in the order without so much as looking in her direction, intensifying Sadie's feeling of solitude in the midst of the crowd. She eyed the distance back to the table she'd come from, but the Blackstones simply took up too much space for her to squeak by without notice.

Then the silence around her registered and she glanced back to realize she'd become the center of attention. Four sets of eyes studied her. Her familiar technique of disappearing into the shadows where she wouldn't be noticed wasn't an option here, as she was boxed in by the wall on one side and the bar counter behind her.

Finally the woman she recognized as Zach's sister stepped closer. "Hi, there. I'm KC, Zach's sister. And you are?"

Sadie wasn't used to people offering her their hands, but she shook anyway. "Sadie Adams."

"Let me guess," KC said with a slight smile. "You must be Zach's new nemesis."

How had she known? "Um…"

"Oh, is this the woman from the mill?" Christina asked, interest lighting her eyes.

Suddenly Sadie felt as though someone had dialed up the spotlight.

"I believe she is," KC replied.

"How did you know?" Sadie asked.

"Honey, it's a small town." KC's smile was friendly, not condescending as Sadie had expected. "Trust me, everybody knows."

"I don't know," Aiden said with a frown.

Christina patted his chest. "I'll fill you in later, dear."

That didn't stop him from studying Sadie in a way that made her more reluctant than ever to stay. But KC picked up her now watered-down drink from the counter and dumped it before starting a fresh one. "Come on over and tell us about yourself," she invited.

Sadie hung on to that friendly smile, even though she knew more than anyone how deceiving it might be from a stranger. But she needed these people for her mission, so she forced her feet forward.

"What do you do, Sadie?" Christina asked.

"I'm a photographer." It wasn't the entire truth. She did take photographs. She just didn't do it for a living, as she'd led them all to believe.

"Oh, where's your camera?"

"Outside." She'd been afraid Zach would make a scene if she brought it in.

Christina didn't seem fazed. "Have you had anything published?"

"Yes, actually. A few pieces through Barnhill Press." The art press wasn't anything to sneeze at, so at least Sadie didn't feel like such a fraud.

Until another voice chimed in. "So you no longer describe yourself as domestic help?"

The people around her froze, unsure how to take Zach's comment. Sadie had no problem with being seen as domestic help. After all, she'd fallen into that category all of her life.

She'd tried to stick as close to the truth as possible. She'd only ever held two things back from Zach the first time around: her employer's true identity and her sister's situation.

Sadie raised her chin and spoke confidently. "Actually, my longtime employer recently passed away. I'm taking a bit of a break before looking for a new position."

"Good luck," Aiden said.

"Thank you." She took a deep breath for courage. "I have an idea I think might interest you."

Suddenly the trio on this side of the bar with her adopted that slightly uncomfortable look that rich people got when they know they were about to be asked for money. She'd seen it often enough back home. But that wasn't what she wanted...

"I wondered if I could have your permission to shoot a series of photographs about the rebuilding of the mill? I visited the town several years ago and became quite attached to it." If they only knew... "From what the people here have been telling me about your family and what you are doing to keep the town alive, well, it's incredible."

She smiled brightly at Christina, since the woman's calm features were easier to focus on. "If nothing else, I think it would make a wonderful memento for the people of the town."

Christina glanced back up at her husband. "Aiden, that sounds wonderful."

"I could talk to the publisher at Barnhill. I've worked with him on several projects...though this would be my first solo proposal," she added, feeling the need to be honest.

On the other side of the bar, she could feel a sense of frustrated resistance coming from Zach. He stared at her, though she refused to meet his gaze. Luckily, she'd already gotten a positive response or she had a feeling he would have blasted her before his employer, simply to keep her from getting close.

Though he still didn't know how close she planned to be...

KC must have sensed it, too, because she kept glancing sideways at her brother. But she didn't speak. Finally Aiden said, "That does sound good. I am a bit worried about safety issues—"

Before he or Zach could go further, she cut him off. "Not a problem. I've already seen the destruction at the mill, and I would definitely need someone to steer me in the safest direction. Someone local, with a lot of experience with the area who could introduce me to people who know the history, the ins and outs of the area. The people and places that make Black Hills so special…"

"That's a great idea," Christina enthused.

Jake and Aiden were nodding along with her. "Definitely," Aiden said. "Zach fits both those criteria and as head of security could keep us informed about your project, too. Would that be a problem?"

"Not for me," she assured him.

Only after speaking did she glance at her former lover, whose hard-won mask barely covered the resentment pushing to get out. Sadie wondered if anyone else could see it. Probably not, because they went on talking as if this were a done deal.

Only Zach kept quiet. Good thing he didn't know the whole story. Otherwise, she might have to worry about her safety.

But at least he would learn. She would get what she wanted…no matter what.

Four

"Just what the hell did you think you were doing?"

Sadie quickly suppressed her smile before turning to face Zach's rage. She and she alone knew the depths of despair she'd experienced since the last time she'd walked away from him. But she couldn't have realized she'd be thrilled to see him under any circumstances...including when he looked like he would choke her if he could.

"Who, me?"

Her innocent question only served to incense him even more. The show was quite spectacular, in fact. Zach's skin took on a ruddy color underneath, showcasing the extent of his anger. But a lifetime as help to people who only wanted things to go their way had taught Sadie to take her kicks where she could get them, even if she could only feel her amusement on the inside.

"You knew I didn't want to spend time with you. So why would you set this whole thing up?" he growled.

Ouch. That hurt, but she had known the way he felt before he even said it. "Look," she said, not afraid to push back. "You started this with your high and mighty attitude, not me."

"So this is all a game to you?" He waved a hand at the damaged building behind him. "This is not a game to these people. This place was their life."

"Yes, and I think it will mean a lot to them to have someone document its resurrection, don't you?"

She wasn't wrong in this. Knowing how much people got attached to places—like she had to Sheldon Hall, even though it would never be hers—gave her a glimpse of exactly how these townspeople felt. "Building positive memories will help shore up the community and keep people here. Isn't that what you want?"

She could see on his face that there wasn't a right answer. He did want that, but it meant spending time with her. Though the reality made her chest ache, she had a job to do just as much as he did. With just as much at stake.

Through clenched teeth Zach brushed her off. "I don't have time to mess with you right now. The fire marshal is here. Just go back to the B and B."

As he stalked across the parking lot, she couldn't help needling him a little more. "I can get some exteriors, though, right?" she called.

He might as well have flipped her the bird, considering the glare on his face. But he held his temper in a gentlemanly way, at least in the midst of the crowd of people he now walked through.

Sadie chuckled, simply because crying in front of everyone wasn't an option, either. She'd suspected that coming back here would be tough, but she could never have imagined the roller coaster of dealing with her own emotions while matching wits with Zach.

Ever comforted by her camera, Sadie set off around the perimeter, once more trying to capture the compound from angles that showcased both the tragedy but also the potential for rebuilding, because that was exactly what people needed to see.

Just a few minutes in, a bell sounded. Glancing around, Sadie saw numerous soot-covered men exit the site and make their way across the parking lot to a couple of huge tents that had been erected along the far edge near the fencing. Must be lunchtime.

After taking a few shots of the men, she edged away from the crowd. Her focus here was pictures, not food.

"Hey, there," a voice said from behind her a few minutes later.

Sadie sighed but finished up her shot before easing her camera down from her face. Had Zach sent another security guard to escort her away today? If so, he was going to have a hell of a fight on his hands.

Turning without any rush, she eyed the man behind her. There was no badge attached to his clothing, and he didn't look dirty like most of the men here. A buttoned-down shirt and Dockers weren't really appropriate attire for a disaster site. But at least he looked friendly.

"Hi," she said, her unease calming down a notch.

"Is that a Canon Mark III body?"

Warmth spread through her. A fellow photographer, maybe? "Yes, with a custom lens. You know it?"

"Ah, I admire from afar and spend my budget on paper and ink instead." The man grinned, looking young despite his thinning hair, and held out his hand. "I'm Lance Parker, editor of the local paper."

She met his hand for a firm shake. "Nice to meet you, Lance. I'm Sadie."

"You must be getting some good pictures, then."

Pulling the camera from around her neck, she clicked on the picture preview and turned the screen so they both could see.

Fifteen minutes of talking cameras and photo composition and lighting fed Sadie's artistic soul. None of her family were interested in photography. She had few friends because of all her responsibilities, but she had managed to join an artists' group near home that she tried to go to once a month.

Sometimes it worked out, sometimes not. But she tried to get her fix in when she could.

"Would it be possible for me to use a couple of these in the newspaper?" he asked. "We'd compensate you, of course. These are wonderful and my two photographers are busy with the cleanup, which keeps them from snapping away right now."

Sadie barely had a chance to think before another voice cut in. "Hey, Lance. How's it going?"

She looked over the newspaper editor's shoulder to see Zach's sister, KC, approaching them. Lance smiled as she arrived.

"As good as can be expected, I think." He gestured to Sadie. "Just trying to convince Sadie here to share a few of her pictures with the community. They would be a great accompaniment to the recovery stories."

KC studied Sadie for a split second, but then her lashes swept down, shielding the expression in eyes so like Zach's. "That would be cool. So, Sadie, what do you think?"

That I don't like being put on the spot... "Yeah, I'll come by and we can look over them again. Tomorrow?"

"Great," KC said, as if she'd decided the subject was closed. "Now y'all want some lunch?"

Lance agreed enthusiastically, but Sadie shook her head. "I'm still full from the breakfast spread my landlady puts out, but I'd be happy to volunteer, if you'd like?"

KC's raised brow and hesitant "Sure" didn't make Sadie feel better. She knew it didn't really matter what KC thought of her, whether she approved. Sadie wouldn't be sticking around Black Hills long enough to make real friends…or sisters-in-law. Somehow that didn't stop her from wishing differently.

Although KC might be hesitant for completely different reasons. Had Zach told her about Sadie? How much did she really know?

Zach made his way back across the parking lot to the food tents KC and Christina had installed. He tried to keep an eye out for Sadie along the way, though he desperately wanted to curse himself for caring where she was in the first place. He could tell himself all he wanted to that it was about suppressing her plans, but deep down he was afraid there were far deeper reasons than that lame excuse.

He didn't see her until he was closer to the tents, and that fiery red hair came into view as she scurried behind the serving line. It wasn't entirely clear from this distance, but it looked almost as if she were in charge.

"Kind of amazing, isn't it?"

Zach glanced to the side to see his little sister approach, her arms filled with a box. He automatically reached for her burden, taking it on himself as he nodded his head in Sadie's direction. "What's going on here?"

KC didn't look at the other woman but continued

to watch her brother…making him very uneasy. "She volunteered to help after saying she wasn't hungry. I could tell she wasn't thrilled with the setup when she joined us, but she didn't say a word."

One side of KC's mouth lifted in a slight smile. "I wondered if she would, but she never did until I started asking for help. It took a few minutes to get her to open up. As soon as she realized she wouldn't offend me by making suggestions, she took the lead. We were whipped into shape in ten minutes and served hundreds in less than half an hour." KC shook her head. "She's good."

Very good. But Zach didn't want to think of that in front of his sister.

"She told me before that she made a living as domestic help, but never went into specifics," he mused as he watched Sadie navigate the chaos with the calm demeanor of a woman who had many pots on the fire but wasn't worried about losing one. He glanced at his sister, only to find her still studying him.

He was in trouble now.

"So you knew her before, as in before this trip to Black Hills?"

Why hadn't he just kept his mouth shut? "Hmm…"

But KC wasn't buying the noncomment. "Did you meet her while you were in the military?"

No, but those days right after he came home had been a blur of nightmares and worry over his mother, his family. He hadn't known how to tell them he was falling in love. After she disappeared without a trace, he'd been glad he kept Sadie to himself and not made her a thing—that thing he had to explain to friends and family, pretend not to miss, or realize hadn't been as real as he'd thought. He had happily done most of that without public scrutiny.

Now, though, he could talk about Sadie without having to get into all the ugliness of regret and pain. He'd never been a liar, but he kept it brief, strictly answering the question that was asked. "No, she's been to town before."

KC slapped her hands to her hips, making him wish he hadn't been gentlemanly enough to take the box. "She was here before, long enough for you to talk to her about her job, and you never mentioned her. Was she a customer? Or—"

"What's for lunch, my lovely?" Jacob's voice interrupted his fiancée's, much to Zach's eternal gratitude.

"Barbecue and fixin's," KC said, giving Jacob a big smile.

"What?" her fiancé's voice boomed over the lot. "Barbecued meat, a pretty lady and a cold beer? All I need is our son and it'll be heaven."

"Christina's got him at the manor," KC said, giving Jacob a quick kiss on the cheek. "Your mom started running a fever this morning, so she stayed home and offered to keep him, too."

Zach saw the flash of concern that crossed Jacob's expression, and knew that even the slightest bug could be very harmful for the Blackstones' mother, who had been in a coma for many years. But KC gave him a reassuring smile.

Jacob pulled her into his arms. "Well, how long is that gonna last? Forget the barbecue. Let's go home."

"Nope, sorry," she said, laughing as she swatted his chest.

Jacob buried his face in KC's neck. "Doomed" was all Zach heard before mumbling and giggling took over. He glanced away, grinning at the two lovebirds' antics. In the sea of chaos under the tent, Sadie stood oddly still. The look on her face, even from this distance, had a hint of sadness and longing before she blinked and it was gone. Actually, all emotion was gone, as if she were afraid for Zach to see too closely inside.

Funny, he felt the same way.

Finally Jacob and KC separated, walking to the food tent hand in hand. Zach fell in step beside them. They talked about the next step in their plan as they joined the dwindling line for food. Sadie certainly had stepped up the efficiency of the process, and now the parking lot was filled with hungry workers eating their fill.

"I'm so glad we could do this," KC said, surveying the scene.

Jacob kissed the top of her head. "Me, too. Whatever it takes to keep Black Hills alive, that's what we're gonna do."

They reached the steam table set up under the tent and chose their meal. Zach deposited the box in the serving area before taking his food tray. Sadie was at the other end in a cute apron with a pig on it, pouring drinks.

"Wow," KC said as she reached Sadie's table. "This was incredible. Thank you so much."

Sadie shrugged away the thanks. "It was no problem."

"No problem? I didn't think so." KC laughed. "Of course, I'm used to a well-ordered kitchen. Being outdoors and not knowing where everything is throws me off."

"Organization is key," Sadie said with a wink.

Jacob reached out to shake Sadie's hand. "Well, we are extremely grateful for your organizational skills."

Sadie shifted as if their praise made her uncomfortable. "I'm glad I could help," she said, handing him a large iced tea.

"Would you be free tomorrow to help some more?" Jacob asked.

Sadie blinked. "I'm sure I can," she said. "I'll be out here tomorrow to take more pictures anyway."

"Did you get any good shots today?" KC asked.

"Sure did."

Jacob looked over at Zach in a way that made him distinctly uneasy. He kept looking. Zach could see the wheels turning.

"Tomorrow," Jacob finally said, "we have a truck coming in with lots of supplies for the workers. Decent boots, heavy overalls, protective gloves and such."

Oh, no. *Jacob, please don't do this to me.*

Jacob didn't even glance in his direction. But his jaw twitched as if he were aware of Zach's dread… and amused by it.

"We need some help getting everything organized and out to the employees. I don't want them working cleanup without good-quality gear."

Zach looked at Sadie in enough time to see her eyes widen. "Isn't that costing a lot for a company that's not bringing in any money at the moment?"

Jacob nodded. "But we want them safe. Those that opted to stay on through the temporary closing and rebuilding are being paid wages to help with cleanup and reconstruction.

"We wanted to keep the work local, as much as possible," Jacob said, his tone firm. "We've got some donations, but everything else is at Blackstone expense. Ultimately, this is about the good of the town. The people who live here deserve to be able to stay."

KC chimed in. "Not be run from their homes by a crazy person."

"That's commendable," Sadie said.

"Not really," Jacob responded, giving her a puzzled look.

"Trust me." She met his look without wavering. "I've known some businessmen who couldn't care less about anything but their bottom line. They'd bring in the cheapest labor and not care who lost their livelihoods. Y'all are doing good here."

Zach could see Sadie mulling all this over, her

brain working in overdrive even though she didn't ask any more questions. She simply picked at the puzzle, trying to unravel the complicated strands.

The fact that he could discern this made him uneasy. He didn't want to read Sadie's mind. Didn't want to feel her curiosity, her disbelief that the Blackstones were good people who cared about their workers. What had happened in her life to lead her to question that?

No, he didn't want to know.

"Sadie, if your organizing skills make this as easy as serving lunch, we'll be in business in no time. Zach will be here when the truck arrives in the morning around nine. He can make sure whatever you need is carried out."

Sure I will. Don't ask me what I want.

Then Zach wondered if his thoughts were showing on his face, because his sister was watching him— very closely.

Sadie, on the other hand, looked pretty pleased with herself. Considering how he'd treated her since she came back to town, he had to wonder why.

As his sister and Jacob moved on, Sadie smiled over at him. "Looks like it's you and me together— again."

Was that a statement…or a threat?

Five

"It's the truth, I tell ya."

Sadie couldn't help but grin at the man before her. Wearing the traditional farmer uniform of overalls, plaid shirt, ball cap and messy white hair, he was a perfect candidate for sitting on a bench in the town square. So were the other two grandfatherly types with him. But he was the talker.

"I think you're pulling my leg," Sadie insisted, knowing it would spur him on.

"No, I would never," he said with a sincere shake of his head. "But I betcha they're all in on it. The other cotton industries are pressuring the state to shut us down, because they want the business we've always had here. That's why all of this is happening."

She knew old men were prime candidates to become conspiracy theorists. They had too much time to sit around and think and talk and spin events into the way they wanted to see them. So she asked, "But Blackstone Mills has been here since the town started, hasn't it?"

"And still putting out quality product," one of the other men, Earl, said. "That's why they have to put us out of business."

Well, as much as she'd like to brush them off, the fact that a bomb had exploded here couldn't be denied. That was deliberate malice, so someone definitely had it in for Blackstone Mills. And the police weren't talking yet.

"I still don't understand why anyone would want to put you out of business," she said, hoping to get more gossip. "Wouldn't someone local have to be in on this? Have access to the plant?"

"Oh, they were," Mr. Farmer breathed.

"The other textile companies found someone local to do their dirty work, we're pretty sure," Earl said.

Farmer interrupted, "We heard about all kinds of things. Can't keep stuff like that secret. Equipment failure and missing shipments. But it was the cotton that was the kicker."

Now they were getting somewhere. Sadie forgot about the lines of men behind her, getting loaded up by fellow workers with their safety gear after she'd streamlined the process for them. Zach had introduced her to the lead volunteer then disappeared, which she was grateful for now, because she was pretty sure these old-timers wouldn't be speaking to her with him around.

Especially about the damaged cotton crop her landlady had mentioned.

"What about the cotton?" she asked, pretending ignorance.

"Oh, that Zachary Gatlin boy did it," Earl said, "though the police said he was innocent."

"We aren't so sure," Farmer said. "He's in thick with those Blackstones, so..." He shrugged. "Why they'd want to damage their own business would be a mystery, but then again, there's a lot about all this that is."

Sadie nodded.

"But he sprayed the cotton, that's all we know. Either somebody loaded the poison in or he did it himself."

"Now he's heading up recovery efforts, so who knows."

"But poison the cotton, it did. Took a while, but they managed to get cotton in from elsewhere. Thank goodness, or the mill would have gone under by Christmas, for sure."

It was the same story she'd heard from her landlady. Something didn't add up, though. "Maybe somebody was trying to frame him?" she mused.

"Frame who?"

The voice from behind her had her stiffening. There was nothing like being caught red-handed talking about someone by the person in question. The men's wide eyes clued her in to their awareness of Zach's presence. Too bad she hadn't been watching them while she was overthinking.

Quickly, she twisted around. "Zach, there you are. I was wondering what happened to you."

Under his breath, so only she could hear, he said, "Didn't sound like it."

Her cheeks flushed hot, but she didn't tuck her chin down the way she wanted to. *Don't show weakness.* Always her first line of defense against the world.

"Gentlemen," he said, glancing over her shoulder. "Glad to see you here. Thanks for supporting us." Then he clasped her elbow. "If you'll excuse us."

He pulled her away, quickly enough that she had to double her short steps to keep up. Looking back, she noticed the men talking and laughing. Goodness only knew what they thought he wanted with her, but whatever their assumption, they thought it was amusing.

Not breaking stride, Zach marched her around the side of the parking area to a more isolated spot before turning to face her. "What was that about?"

"What do you mean?" She had a feeling her innocent look wasn't going to work here.

She was right.

"What right do you have to talk about me, about my life, with the people of this town?"

"Well, technically the conversation didn't start out that way—"

"I don't care how it started." His voice rose enough to sting her ears. "Just that it stops. Now."

Unbidden, Sadie could feel her backbone stiffening and her expression becoming a blank mask. A lifetime in service had taught her how to deal with difficult people, usually men, and their expressions of displeasure. She instinctively took steps to protect herself, even if walking away from the situation wasn't an option. Which it usually wasn't.

Her voice was awfully formal when she spoke. "I'm sorry you feel that way, but I was simply asking about the mill and they offered information. I didn't dig into anything."

"I heard you asking questions."

She narrowed her eyes at him. If he thought she would just take this, he was mistaken. He didn't know her as well as he thought. "A question. You heard me ask a question about you, and that's after Earl brought you up." She cocked her head to the side. "But I do have another question."

"I'm not telling you anything about myself." His snarl said she didn't deserve it.

Which she didn't. "And thus my question. Why do you care if I ask?"

Zachary Gatlin hated being caught off guard. He'd spent his military career planning for the unexpected, but that didn't mean he liked it.

Luckily, Sadie didn't wait for an answer.

"Look," she said, "I have to ask questions. How else am I gonna know what to take pictures of? Who to take pictures of? Talking to people is part of that."

She cocked her jeans-clad hip, the hand she propped there drawing his eye more than he liked. "If that's a problem, I can do it on my own. After all, you are only supposed to escort me through the mill."

"No," he said through clenched teeth. Not just from his anger, either. Being only a foot away from her seemed to be causing his entire body to go haywire. "That's not what Jacob meant, and you know it."

"I know nothing of the sort." Her brows rose. He didn't remember her being so sassy before. This time she was pushing all his buttons. "I only know that the mill is dangerous right now and they want you with me when I go inside. That's the only sure thing."

"It's my job to make sure *everything* you go over is safe." They both knew what his emphasis meant, even if she wanted to pretend otherwise.

"Then I guess you'd better stick a little closer, don't you think?"

For a split second, that sassy pink mouth and raised brow made Zach drop his protective barriers. Without thought, he stepped in. Her back hit the wall behind her. His hand planted right above her shoulder. There was barely a hand's breadth between their chests. Their lips were even closer.

Zach's heart moved into double time. *Remain im-*

passive. But he couldn't when his entire body was straining to press in close and make contact in the most primitive way he knew how. *Touch.*

Their breath mingled. He allowed one point of contact. Only one, when he wanted so many more. He reached out with his other hand and curled it around her waist, soaking in the warmth of her body beneath the T-shirt she wore.

"Oh, I'm gonna stick pretty damn close, sweetheart," he said, relishing her eyes going wide with something akin to nerves. "I'll be keeping an eye on every move you make. Every word you speak. Every picture you take." No matter how creepy that might be.

He could be dedicated to his job, couldn't he? "No more snooping behind my back."

"Roger that," she whispered.

It was the barest brush of her lip against his that broke the hold she had over his body. That accidental contact shook him to his core—which was the last thing he wanted her to know. So he stepped back. Removed his hand. Controlled his breathing.

And met her gaze. He could have sworn she'd just gotten exactly what she wanted.

Which filled his mind with images of other times she'd gotten what she wanted, only they were much more intimate things, things he didn't want to remember when he was standing this close to her.

Then she threw him off guard again. "I'm sorry," she whispered.

Zach blinked, not switching gears fast enough. "What?"

"I'm sorry that you're angry with me."

He met her eyes, studying their green depths, not sure if he wanted to go back to the time when he'd known her before. But his body spoke before his mind could catch up. "But you're not sorry you left?"

Her expression flattened, her pale skin going almost white. The spare sprinkle of freckles on her cheeks stood out in contrast. "I didn't have a choice," she finally said.

"Zach?" someone called before he could push for more. He forced himself to pull back, to let his arm fall to his side, to clench his teeth together so he wouldn't ask why. Then he deliberately turned his head to the side, blocking her out.

Because he didn't need to know why. Knowing that she had walked away was more than enough.

Six

"Zach, are you ready?"

Sadie tore her gaze from Zach to look at Jacob Blackstone, who stood about five feet from them. To her embarrassment, she had to blink a moment before her gaze would focus on him. Instead she wanted nothing more than to turn back to Zach and press her lips to his. No matter who was looking.

So close.

But Zach wouldn't be there waiting. He strode toward his future brother-in-law, not looking back. "Yeah, I'm ready."

"Ready for what?" she asked.

"They've cleared us to take a preliminary tour inside before the workers go into the parts of the building that were damaged to start cleanup."

She glanced at Zach's retreating back. For someone who said he wasn't letting her out of his sight, he sure was moving away at a fast clip.

"Are you coming?" Jacob asked. Sadie found herself on the receiving end of his inquisitive look.

"Yes, if I may," she said. Apparently, Zach wasn't so far away he hadn't heard that, because his shoulders had straightened, hard.

Jacob led her back to the trailer and got some boots and coveralls in her size. Once she was dressed and had collected her camera, she approached the men again where they stood with two soot-covered figures with clipboards. She steeled herself as Zach turned toward her, but he held out a bright yellow hard hat. "This, too," he said simply.

Jacob introduced her to the fire inspectors, then they headed for the building entrance. To her surprise, a large group of workmen formed a crowded semicircle near the door. Jacob paused to shake a few hands and speak, but the still, respectful patience of the hundred or so people brought out an emotional response in Sadie.

She wasn't used to this. She had more experience with the spoiled variety of the human species. But the simple look on their faces told her this place meant something to them. When Jacob gave the word that it was time, they'd put their backs into rebuilding it—paycheck or no.

Stepping back, she got some wide-angle shots of the crowd, then the entrance. As she took her turn stepping through, her chest tightened. To be the first to see the destruction of this place felt significant. And this wasn't even the worst part of the damage. Her hold on her camera got a little tighter. Hopefully she'd be able to do her subject some justice.

The smell of smoke lingered in the air outside the building, but it hadn't prepared her for the thickness of it inside. It seemed to immediately dry out her throat and threaten to choke her. She found herself panting, trying to limit the air's access to her lungs.

The outer rooms were relatively intact except for their blackened walls, but as they traveled deeper, more damage began to appear. Bubbled paint, peeled portions of Sheetrock, black marks following trails that she assumed were electrical wires in the walls.

"Wow," said a masculine voice near her.

Sadie turned her head to see a big bear of a man staring down the hallway. The hard movement of his Adam's apple told her just how much seeing this affected him.

The rest of the group that had come in were just ahead, leaving Sadie and the man behind a bit. "What did you do here?" she asked.

There was no doubt he had worked here. Someone didn't view a building, especially an industrial building, with such emotion if there wasn't a personal tie.

He turned to her as if he hadn't realized she was there. He blinked rapidly. She knew the feeling well.

Working in Sheldon Hall for the Beddingfield family, she'd learned early on all the tricks to hiding those telltale signs of emotion. Instead of pushing, she waited to see if he was interested in talking to her or wanted to be left alone.

Once under control, he offered a halfhearted smile. "Oh, I'm Bateman, the day shift foreman."

She snapped a few pictures of the group ahead of them, getting a long-range perspective, so the foreman wouldn't feel as if she was too focused on him. "So you must have worked here a long time to reach that position," she surmised.

"Since I was a young'un," he said, and this time his smile was more genuine. She smiled back, her heart softening even more.

He went on. "I was hired by the old Mr. Blackstone himself. I tell you, I about wet my pants that day."

"Intimidating?"

"Oh, yes," he said, moving forward once more. "He was a fierce one. I just happened to get lucky— or unlucky, as it were. The hiring manager was sick the day of my interview. But I must have passed muster, because he hired me on the spot. I was seventeen."

They picked their way down halls, pausing beside rooms with water and smoke damage. Sadie managed some more artistic photos of the damage, along with pictures of Bateman while he surveyed the areas. The deeper they journeyed into the building, the harder it became for Sadie to breathe, though she tried not to let it show. Her body felt hot, as if it could still feel the flames, even though she knew that was impossible.

The effects of the explosion became more evident as they proceeded. Sadie could tell they were coming closer to the heart of the plant. Closer to the connection to the admin building where the bomb had been placed. Here pieces of the ceiling were missing; what parts of the walls were left were completely charred and the smoke lay like a blanket over them.

Bateman paused just inside the entrance to a long, cavernous room. As Sadie paused next to him, she noticed the remnants of two-by-fours that had once formed wall dividers, the twisted metal remnants of filing cabinets against the far walls. This room had once been either offices or cubicles. At the far end of the room, the group of men ahead of them also paused. Sadie tried not to watch but couldn't miss Zach's proud bearing and confident interactions with those around him.

Her heart ached, even if she didn't want to acknowledge it. So she turned back to Bateman.

"Since seventeen? That is a long time."

Bateman's smile was tinged with something sad. "Yes, I've been here a long time. My sons work here. And last year my grandson came to work here, too."

"Your family is very important to you."

"Always." Again she saw that sheen of tears, though he tried to hide it by turning his face in the other direction. "If this place closes, what will happen to us? We've always been close. But they're already looking for jobs elsewhere."

Sadie rarely found herself in this position in her day job, but she'd spent more than her fair share of time in hospitals. Her natural compassion asserted itself. She couldn't help patting his arm, though she pretended not to see his tears. Grown men almost always preferred it that way.

"I don't think that will be necessary," she said, hoping her words would soothe him. "From the sounds of it, the Blackstones are gonna do everything they can to keep that from happening."

In her peripheral vision, she saw Bateman blink several times and nod. To give him more privacy, she glanced back at the other men—and found Zach's dark stare trained on her.

This time, she couldn't look away. She felt almost paralyzed by the intensity, as if by sheer will he could see deep inside her.

And for once, she wished she could show him.

Suddenly the connection broke as Zach glanced up and his eyes widened. "Watch out," he yelled.

Sadie quickly followed his example and looked at the ceiling. Her mind barely registered some kind of debris falling before she flung her hands out to push Bateman away.

It happened fast. She pushed. Bateman pulled. Pain slashed across her cheek. The camera shattered.

They both went down, then Sadie saw stars across her field of vision before everything went blank.

"Really, I'm fine."

Zach watched as Sadie went a few rounds with the nurse in the temporary first aid center they had set up.

"No, you're not. That cut needs stitches," the nurse, Marty, said.

If anything, Sadie paled even more. "Just butterfly it."

"And mar that gorgeous face forever?" The young guy was aghast. And no, that slinky dark emotion wheedling into Zach was not jealousy—or any form of territorial assertion. "No, ma'am."

As others crowded the opening behind him, Zach turned to KC and Jacob, who both wore concerned expressions. "How is she?" KC whispered.

Zach answered at the same volume, for some reason not wanting Sadie to know they were talking about her. "Very unhappy in the face of treatment." An unusually strong panic had graced her features every time any mention was made of going to the hospital. She seemed to only want to go back to the B and B and pretend she was fine. Zach did not care for the curiosity leaking into his thoughts. "And she'll be even more unhappy when she realizes what happened to her camera."

There was a general chorus of winces before the nurse joined their little group. "She'll need some stitches for that cut on her face. The hard hat did its job. Still, I'd feel better if she wasn't gonna be alone tonight. Especially once she's got some pain meds in her."

There were a lot of logical solutions to this problem. Sadie could stay at Blackstone Manor with Aiden and Christina. After all, Christina was a nurse. But she was pregnant and Ms. Blackstone, the brothers' mother, had been fighting some kind of infection lately.

KC—or hell, even Zach's mother—could take care of Sadie overnight.

So why did he hear himself saying, "I'll do it."

He ignored the myriad glances that swung his way. "She'll be more comfortable at the B and B with her own stuff," he said, offering a fairly reasonable excuse. "And I'm the only single person with no kids in this bunch."

Marty gave him a nod, as if this were the given option. "I'll get some instructions put together, but I imagine you know what warning signs to look for?"

He sure did. Zach's military background had trained him for this and a whole lot more. Unfortunately, he'd had to put that knowledge into practice a time or two. Times he'd prefer to not just forget but to completely obliterate from his memory.

Marty went back to his patient and the others talked quietly together in that intimate way couples had. Zach watched as Bateman lumbered in across the small space. He knelt by Sadie's chair, the movement oddly humble in a man his size.

Sadie smiled at the older man, then immediately winced. As they talked, Zach thought back to earlier, to Sadie's comforting hand on Bateman's arm, to her push to get him out of the direct path of the falling debris... All those things matched the Sadie he remembered from before she'd pulled her disappearing act.

The new Sadie had been more of a challenge, demanding, secretive almost—instead of just sweet. He didn't want to be intrigued, yet he was.

What had brought on those changes? Obviously there was some of that sugary-sweet woman in there somewhere—so where had the new spice come from?

Zach suddenly realized Sadie was staring at him, her big moss-green eyes uncertain and almost fearful. The nurse must have told her about tonight's sleeping arrangements. He didn't care if it was the coward's way out; he made a quick exit.

There was still work to do—and if it helped him avoid any questions, all the better.

But he couldn't avoid Sadie a couple of hours later as he drove her slightly dopey self back to the B and B. He'd gotten her key before they'd left the mill.

When they went inside, there was no nosy landlady in the lobby to ask too many questions. Sadie leaned into him on the stairs. He told himself it would be rude to make her climb them on her own in her current shaky state. If only he could just ignore the softness of her body as it pressed against his—in such an achingly familiar fit. The light caramel scent of her hair stirred an all-too-base hunger. He felt the echo of anticipation from another time when he had been leading her to bed.

No matter how many times he told himself it couldn't happen between them again, his urges were steadily drowning out the voice of reason.

"You don't have to do this," Sadie said in the same sexy drawl that featured in his memories of that one emotion-charged night five years ago.

"I take my job very seriously," he said as he unlocked her room and led her inside.

"I see that," she said, swaying slightly where she stood. Apparently Sadie couldn't handle pain meds very well. "You've always gone above and beyond."

Zach didn't deny it. That was a part of his nature he couldn't get rid of. Whether he was writing a grocery list, doing a job or taking care of his family, he was usually in whole hog.

A cute frown scrunched up Sadie's usually open features. "But I can take care of myself," she said. She shuffled toward the dresser. "After all, I've been doing it all my life."

He refrained from pointing out that she would have been driving impaired if he had let her go home alone, and watched her pull out pajamas. She shuffled to what he assumed was the bathroom and shut herself inside.

Right, he'd conveniently forgotten about the stubborn streak.

Dropping the overnight bag he kept stowed in his SUV, Zach strolled over and sank onto the couch to wait, banging his knee against the little coffee table in the process. The laptop before him sprang to life.

Four pictures filled the screen, all of him. These weren't the classic survey pictures he was used to seeing. Each one was artistically composed with strategic lighting and showed him absorbed in some task. Except for the one in the bottom right corner, in which he stared straight ahead with a sad look on his face.

The pictures had an indefinable quality portraying not just his emotion but the photographer's as well. Almost a wistful, yearning feel.

Looking at them, it hit him—Sadie had missed him after all.

The bathroom door opened. Somehow, Zach knew Sadie would not want him to see these pictures. With a flick of his wrist, he closed the laptop.

He looked away so he could avoid seeing the sway of her breasts beneath the short, fitted nightie she wore. Unlike the oversize T-shirts his sister had preferred as a teenager, Sadie was all girl when it came to pajamas and underwear.

Nope. Don't go there.

She plopped onto the bed then dropped back onto a mound of pillows. The minute her head made contact, she winced.

But her sleepy eyes met his defiantly. "See. I'm good."

Yes, you are. He smothered a smile. "Sure you are."

She ignored him, rolling onto her side. He could have been offended at her presenting her back, except he knew from experience that was the side she slept on.

He stood for a long time in the middle of the room, almost able to pinpoint to the second when she sank into sleep. His gaze traced the familiar S curve of her body he was desperate to curl around once more. He looked out the window at the darkening sky, then at the alarm screen on his phone that told him when he would need to wake her next.

And finally, the laptop.

He didn't have to open it to know what was inside. Those pictures were imprinted on his brain. Mixed with the yearning he'd seen on her face when they'd stood in the alley this morning, he knew deep inside that Sadie still wanted him, too.

Then he stripped down to his boxer briefs and climbed into bed beside Sadie. At some point, his body made up his mind for him. He might be a selfish bastard, but if this was his chance to have one more taste of the only woman who had tempted his heart, he wasn't going to turn it down.

Seven

Waking to the feel of strong arms and Zach's scent wasn't unusual for Sadie. He remained in her dreams no matter how many days they were apart. She let herself hover there between wakefulness and sleep, wishing the feel of him would never disappear.

Ever so slowly, the mist started to recede. "Zach," she whispered, her mind still not comprehending. "Zach, is that you?"

"Yes," he murmured. "I'm here."

"Please don't leave me."

"I didn't leave you. You left me."

"But I never really wanted to."

Only the sudden stiffening of the body beside hers awakened her enough to realize that he was real rather than a figment of her imagination. So warm and alive she could have wept in gratitude.

The confusion dissipated in a rush of fever as desire swept through her. She'd denied her need for too long.

His groan filled the air. The rough scratch of hair and smooth heat of skin graced her palms, telling her she had reached out to touch. To test whether the apparition of her dreams was indeed real.

And that's when reality returned in an unwelcome rush.

She shouldn't. She knew she shouldn't, that deep down it made what she was doing that much more despicable. Her betrayal then, and her betrayal now.

Her fingers curled, digging into the warm flesh as if to keep him with her just a moment longer. His quick catch of breath signaled a change in the air, a breach of a barrier that shouldn't be forgotten.

But it was too late.

Her mind cried out with joy as his body rolled against hers, sweeping over her to take control. He was the same Zach she remembered. His familiar scent and bulk enveloped her. Her need exploded deep inside. For this moment she would let go of the past, not worry about the future and do the one thing Sadie never did: enjoy the present.

For the first time in five years, she felt his lips against hers. Not the barely there brush from the mill, but a full meeting of lips that conveyed passion and want. Sadie's palms found the bare skin of his shoulders, tracing muscles bulked by years of true labor. For long moments his lips distracted her. It wasn't the tentative touch of new lovers, but the eager reunion, the rediscovery of each other.

Just as her hands traced sinewy muscle over his ribs, he dipped down. The heat radiating from him blanketed her, left her aching for more. She wanted freedom—freedom from her clothes, from her fear, from the secrets that stood between them.

The tips of his hair, much longer than the last time they were together, brushed her cheeks. It tickled, lightening her mood a little. She smiled against his lips. Her hands automatically burrowed into the silky strands, and she savored the thickness, the new weight that signaled his complete return to civilian life.

Her hands in his hair ramped up something for him, because his movements took on a frantic edge. A powerful purpose that plunged her into heaven.

He stripped her of her nightgown, then panties. His thighs settled between hers as he assumed possession. Then he traced her ribs with his palms, reminding her of the first time his hands had explored her body.

Time coalesced in a surreal effect, mixing this moment with a night five years ago when Zach had introduced her to an ecstasy she'd only ever dreamed of before. Now, as then, he touched every part of her as if committing her body to memory. Fingers kneading her muscles. Nails stimulating her skin. Palms controlling her hips.

From somewhere deep inside her a whimper erupted. His hands tightened at the sound, keeping her from lifting against him. The inability to move only ramped up her need. Her core melted in liquefied heat.

Suddenly his warmth receded as he crouched between her thighs. It took a moment of disoriented disappointment to realize he hadn't left her. Then he pressed his open mouth to her thigh. She tensed. Each sucking kiss brought him closer to the apex of her need, but never close enough. Her gasps filled the silence.

Just when she'd thought he would end her suffering, his mouth moved to her belly button, then out along her ribs. This time her breath caught, then she giggled at his touch. He growled, his approval obvious as he rediscovered every spot that made her laugh, sigh and moan.

Finally he stretched out over her once more. He buried his hands in her hair. The long strands wound around his fingers, and he took full advantage, tugging until her chin lifted. Sadie wanted to weep as control and guilt swept away from her. All she could do was enjoy.

His kiss against her neck was firm, demanding. This time there was no stopping her hips from lifting, her hands from clutching him to her. His mouth worked its magic while his other hand guided his hardness to her. The stretch right to the edge of fullness made her wince. It had been so long.

Too long.

But her nails dug into the cheeks of his ass, pulling him into her with devastating effect. Her entire body exploded into tingles as he moved within her. It was exactly as she remembered, and so much more.

His body demanded her response. She gave him her all. Hips clashing. Skin rubbing. Breath mingling. Until the night erupted into a million points of light and emotion.

Cementing her to him...forever.

Zach's eyes opened when he heard the click of the bathroom door the next morning...then the unmistakable turn of the lock.

In the military he'd trained himself to be instantly alert upon awakening, but the habit wasn't always beneficial in civilian life. For instance, at the moment, his clear mind began to play last night over and over and over again. Which wasn't what he wanted.

The feelings and memories urged him to get his naked ass out of bed and into the shower with her. If only he hadn't heard the telltale sound of the lock shutting him out.

So instead he covered his naked ass with a clean pair of jeans and headed downstairs for some coffee. At least he didn't run into the proprietress first thing—which was good for her. He wasn't in the mood to deal with Gladys before getting in a good shot of caffeine. The breakfast room was empty, though there were pans of fresh rolls and biscuits on the sideboard, and the dark smell of his favorite breakfast brew permeated the room.

The hot black coffee distracted him from what he would say to Sadie when she appeared, what he would do from this point onward.

Her agreement with the Blackstones meant he couldn't ignore her, couldn't get away. She hadn't been the clingy type—now or in the past. But he could honestly say this wasn't a situation he was used to being in with women.

His relationships since he'd been home from the air force had been few and far between. They weren't really relationships, per se. Life had been too full of obligations and change to indulge in something that required that level of commitment—and he'd never felt the urge for more than a good time.

Except with Sadie.

A flicker of movement in his peripheral vision had him looking to the doorway. Sadie straightened her gray sweater, smoothing it down over jeans-clad hips in the barest flicker of nerves. Then she continued into the room and joined him at his table. Her smile was artificial, but it highlighted the bow curve of her upper lip—the same lip that had felt so soft and hungry beneath his own the night before.

"Are you hungry?" Sadie asked quietly, tentatively testing the waters. "Gladys's husband makes some incredible cinnamon rolls."

"I'm definitely not a man to turn down good food. My mama will testify to that," he said.

She waved him back as he started to rise, so he watched as she filled two plates with rolls and some fruit. Then she lifted a large metal lid and the smell of meat filled the air. She added a couple of slices of bacon to his plate. She'd remembered. He was an avid bacon lover.

Had she learned that so well in the week they'd danced around each other before giving in to their passion?

She laid the plate before him in silence, then fixed her own cup of coffee, doctored with sugar and a liberal dose of cream. This was a natural rhythm that he'd noticed from her before. Just like at the mill, where efficiency in a large-scale task seemed routine for her, so he'd also found her to take charge of these little, everyday domestic tasks, too. Not in an overbearing way, but with a calm efficiency that matched her approach to life in general—at least, as far as Zach could tell.

And probably a way to make herself more comfortable around here.

After she was seated, she drew a long sip from the blue-glazed pottery mug. He munched on bacon, but theirs wasn't a comfortable silence. He sensed Sadie wanted to say something, and wondered idly if he was facing the Dear John conversation he hadn't been subjected to the last time. Odd how the thought bothered him.

He would have preferred not to care one way or another.

"I didn't plan on that, you know," she said, her usual quiet, even tone belying the anxiety with which she stared at her food.

"I know." He noticed the slight puffiness along her upper cheekbone and the fresh bandage on her cheek.

She took another sip, her gaze still trained on her plate.

The least he could give her was honesty. "Neither did I. That wasn't why I brought you home."

Suddenly her gaze snapped up, and he found himself entranced by her brilliant green eyes. How could such a clear color hide so many secrets from him?

They both started as something heavy landed on the table. Zach had been so lost in their stilted conversation that he hadn't noticed the approach of Gladys. He glanced up, sure his expression portrayed just how much he appreciated her intrusion.

"Why, Sadie, you didn't mention you would have a visitor for…breakfast."

The overly long pause told Zach that Gladys was fishing. She must not have noticed him making his way downstairs earlier—surprising for a woman who seemed to know everything.

"Sorry, Gladys," Sadie said.

"Well, how lucky for me that it's Zachary Gatlin."

Zachary couldn't imagine a time when Gladys had ever been that happy to see him, except when she hoped to get a juicy bit of gossip. He looked up with an arched brow. This might be more interesting than he'd thought. "And why would that be?" Zach didn't believe in beating around the bush.

"Why, I get to be the first to congratulate you."

"On what, exactly?" There hadn't been a lot happening worthy of celebration lately.

"On being officially cleared for the cotton poisoning, of course."

She tapped the newspaper she'd dropped on the table with a well-manicured finger. The top headline read, Founding Family Son Charged in Mill Bombing. Zach was still trying to put the pieces together when Sadie picked up the top section of the paper. Zach didn't need to read it. He already knew who was to blame. Which was a perk of being part of the inner Blackstone circle.

Sadie seemed to be devouring the text. Zach watched her for a moment, then glanced up at Gladys as she continued to stand next to the table.

"Isn't it great, Zach?" she asked with a gleam in her eye that said she couldn't wait to be on the phone the minute she had something to pass along. If he didn't give her something, she'd just make up something interesting. Of course, the fact that Zach was here, and had probably come down from Sadie's room, would be the first thing she'd offer.

"Yes, Gladys. It's very nice."

Even though I shouldn't need the validation of being proven innocent. His sister, his mother, Jacob and his new employers all believed in him, even when the evidence had been totally damning. Those were the people that mattered.

So he kept it simple.

As Gladys headed back to the kitchen with a disappointed look on her face, Zach turned to find Sadie's eyes on his. "Why blow her off like that?"

"Because she's looking for a scoop, something to share with the grapevine."

Sadie nodded. Her guarded expression held a hint of sadness, as if she understood his need to protect himself. But what he really wanted to know was what she hid behind the mask…and whether he would regret last night if he found out her true secrets.

Eight

"I'll finish getting ready."

At least, that's what Sadie told Zach to get a few minutes alone in her room. She needed to make a phone call before Zach took her anywhere this morning. Since her car was still at the mill, she didn't have any choice but to get a few things in order and hitch a ride into town.

Luckily, Zach hadn't pushed anything after their conversation at breakfast. She'd had the distinct impression he'd just as soon step out in the parking lot and get out of ready reach of Gladys. Not that she could blame him.

She was well acquainted with people who blamed first and asked questions later.

Sadie also loved the people who pretended she didn't exist, because it was easier than having to be polite.

Not that she was in a position to judge. As she picked up her phone, she was all too aware of that fact.

"I need a new camera," she said without preamble when Victor picked up.

He wasn't thrilled—not that she'd thought he would be. "What the heck does that have to do with me?" he asked.

Sadie explained how the camera had been shattered when she'd dropped it, then the falling debris had finished the job.

"My question stands."

"A photographer has a camera. A nice camera."

"Then I guess you should have held on to yours."

Why did she bother explaining anything to this guy? "According to our contract, you are responsible for all business expenses, including a camera. I could have considered it a regular expense, but it's not, so I'm actually giving you the courtesy of informing you that you need to pay for it." Sadie had covered every loophole she could think of in the deal with Victor. It was all completely spelled out in black and white. And he'd needed her, so he'd signed.

"So sue me."

"If you don't pay, I'll just have to wait for the insurance claim. They'll take care of it…eventually. But it will mean a delay—"

"Fine. What am I getting for my generosity?"

Nothing he was going to like…but Sadie kept that thought to herself. Better not to antagonize him any more than normal.

"Unfortunately, nothing at the moment. My biggest lead was blown away this morning." She explained how the newspaper article had laid out bombing suspect Mark Zabinski's connection to the local airfield and how his presence there would not have been questioned. This gave the police reason to look into his possible sabotage of the containers on Zach's plane. That meant Zach was innocent, and the crop poisoning couldn't be used to disinherit him. She'd have to find something else. Victor's curses rang in her ear even before she'd finished.

His voice rose in volume and ugliness with every word. "Then find something else. We're running out of time."

The sound of him slamming the phone down made her wince, but to her relief he disconnected the call. Letting her eyelids drift closed, she took a few moments to breathe. Her body and her emotions had been through a lot in the past few days. She was exhausted. Her head hurt. And she had to face the fact that she'd had sex with Zach, knowing good and well she would betray him before her time here was over.

Having to deal with Victor on top of all that was more than she could handle, as evidenced by the tremble in her fingers as she opened her laptop and accessed the internet. By the time she went downstairs to meet Zach outside, she knew exactly where she needed to go next.

"Would you mind if we went out to Callahan's before heading all the way out to the mill?"

Zach threw a glance her way but quickly returned his eyes to the road. "Sure. What do you need there?"

"Mr. Callahan can order a replacement for my camera. I'd prefer to get it done as soon as possible." Who knew what she might get involved in once she got to the mill? Plus, it was a long way from town. By the time she got there and got her car, it could be late afternoon.

If there was one thing Sadie wanted almost as much as Zach, it was her camera. Her fingers ached to curl around it once more. Only another shutterbug would understand the feeling, but it was there nonetheless.

"I was surprised when you dropped it," Zach said, his tone more than conversational somehow. "I knew before that your camera was your baby. This one was really nice."

She wasn't going to pretend she hadn't felt a twinge as it left her hands, because Zach already knew the truth in that. Still, she shrugged. "In the end, it's just a thing." And she knew all too well how little things meant in the long run. "Compared to a person…at least the camera can be replaced."

"Won't that be expensive?"

Goodness, yes. "That's what credit cards are for, I guess. The insurance will eventually pay me back."

Until then, Victor better have it covered.

"Why are we even having this conversation?" she asked, not backing down when Zach shot a glance her way. "Do you really view me as that heartless of a human being that I wouldn't value Mr. Bateman's safety over my camera?"

"No, but—"

"Wouldn't you drop whatever you were holding to push your sister out of the way?"

"Yes, but Bateman is a stranger."

"Who still has a family he cares about and who would miss him if something bad happened to him. You may not approve of all of my actions, Zach, but I still think I'm basically a decent human being."

"One who's grown a pretty decent backbone."

"I told you I was sorry. But I'm not gonna dissolve into sackcloth and ashes or let you whip me with the past. That isn't good for either of us."

She sucked in a breath, suddenly realizing the extent of her tirade. But she couldn't finish without saying, "It won't change it, either, much as I wish it could." Because in the end, honesty was important to her, so she would honor that where and when she could without harming her own family...

Zach didn't respond this time. Sadie's nerves tightened with every turn of the steering wheel, but she wasn't backing down on this.

It wasn't until they reached the little camera shop on one side of the town square that he finally spoke.

"You're right, Sadie. My apologies."

She'd have been happier if his tone hadn't been so formal, but in the end, it was for the best, wasn't it?

The store had a checkered awning that matched numerous others around the old-fashioned square, easily visible now that the leaves were mostly missing from the Bradford pear trees lining the streets. Sadie wondered what cute little Christmas traditions the town observed and whether those bare branches would be wrapped in holiday lights. She wished she could be here to see it, to walk along the sidewalks with Zach and soak in the atmosphere.

But her life was elsewhere. So were the people who were counting on her. She tried not to think about how quickly she might have to leave as she stepped through the door into a camera lover's paradise.

"Hello, my dear Sadie," Mr. Callahan said. "What an unexpected pleasure."

"For me, as well," she said with a smile, allowing the dapper Southern gentleman to press a gentle kiss to her cheek.

She caught a glimpse of Zach's surprised look as she pulled back. Why was he shocked? She'd made more friends than just him when she'd been here before.

"That is quite a large bandage you have there,"

Mr. Callahan remarked. "Did you, by chance, receive that yesterday?"

"Why, yes," Sadie said. "A cut, but it will heal. What I'm really worried about is my camera."

He nodded sagely, reminding her of a benevolent, skinny Santa. "Yes, I heard about that, too."

Well, this was a small town… "I see." After all, what should she say?

Zach wasn't having any difficulty coming up with words. "She was very brave, pushing Bateman out of the way of that falling debris."

For a moment, Sadie wondered why he was so open with Mr. Callahan when he'd practically refused to talk to Gladys at the B and B. But she knew it probably had to do with Mr. Callahan's integrity. He didn't need gossip as a source of entertainment.

"I'm glad you came to see me," he said. "Though there is no hope of repair?"

"Since the camera is sitting under a pile of loose plaster and two-by-fours, I doubt it," Zach answered.

Sadie winced as she remembered her last glimpse of the camera. "I was able to get almost all of my pictures off, since I download them to my laptop every night. But I'll bring in the digital card and see if you can get the ones from that day for me."

The gleam in the older man's eyes said he looked forward to the challenge. "It will be my pleasure."

"Until then, I need to order a new one."

Mr. Callahan moved over to a computer on the counter. "What kind?"

When she told him, he whistled. "You've stepped up in the world," he said.

"And now I'm in deep mourning." It was either brush it off or cry.

"Let's see if we can resurrect it," he said with a wink.

"The Blackstones would appreciate it," Zach said, surprising Sadie. "She's using the camera to create a visual history of the mill's resurrection."

That had the older man's eyes widening. "Are you now? I can't wait to get a sneak peek at the digital card."

"I can bring my laptop down here later this week so you can see what I have so far. The building and people down there make fascinating subjects." Especially certain people. She'd have to make sure those photos were in a completely different folder.

"I imagine so," Mr. Callahan said, even as his fingers continued clicking on the keyboard. "I've always been interested in the juxtaposition of all that steel and metal with endless fields of cotton. From what I saw yesterday when I drove out there, the damage is quite picturesque."

He paused, staring into space for a moment. "Kind of interesting that James Blackstone's empire suffers ruin just over a year after his death."

"Was he the original owner?" Sadie asked.

"The original dictator," Zach scoffed.

Mr. Callahan agreed with a knowing look. "The original business was built several generations ago, and added to through the years, but it was James Blackstone who catapulted it into luxury quality linens."

"So he was a good businessman?" Sadie asked.

Zach was quick to answer. "Yes. And a miserable human being."

She studied his suddenly shuttered face. "That sounds like it comes from personal experience."

He simply shrugged and walked away, leaving her to wonder as he strolled around the length of the old-fashioned, quirky shop.

She glanced over at Mr. Callahan. He gave her a half smile. "I'm not big on telling other people's stories," he said, "but James was most definitely difficult. He ruled Black Hills with an iron fist and had definite views on how things should be done." He, too, glanced over at Zach. "And he wasn't above using devious tactics to get what he wanted, either."

He finished putting Sadie's package together on the computer, checked it twice, then rang up a payment on her card that made her slightly nauseous. If Victor didn't come through with that money in her bank account by tomorrow, she was going to ruin him for sure.

He was used to throwing around that type of money, but Sadie definitely was not.

They headed back out to the car, Mr. Callahan's promise that the camera would be delivered in forty-eight hours drifting behind them.

Hopefully it wouldn't be a moment longer.

There weren't too many things that made Sadie impatient, but waiting on a camera was like a kid anticipating the bike they just knew they would find under the tree Christmas morning.

The silence in the car on the way to the mill wasn't helping her nerves. "So the Blackstone men I've met," she asked, "they're James Blackstone's grandsons?"

Zach nodded.

"You seem to know them well."

"Not really…at least, not until recently. Different circles and all that." The words were accompanied by a smirk, but at least he'd started talking.

"KC actually got involved with Jacob Blackstone first, months before I knew the family. Before that, I just knew *of* them. None of the grandsons lived here then. She met Jacob when he came home on a visit to his mother, and then she ended up pregnant with Carter."

The scowl darkening his features turned fierce. "That was my first up close and personal encounter with the patriarch of the family. He threatened my sister, scared her so badly she left town. I'll never forgive him for that."

Sadie recognized something in Zach's expression all too well. "Or yourself?"

He shot a quick glance her way before resolutely returning his eyes to the road. "She knew I wouldn't have held back. I've spent my life protecting my family. And I would have jeopardized my livelihood and my mother's bar to teach that son of a bitch a lesson." His knuckles whitened from his tight grip. "So she made a decision and left alone. She didn't come back until James was dead."

Zach took a deep breath, almost as if cleansing himself of the memories. "Jacob and KC were lucky. Their story ended in a happily-ever-after—but it never would have if James had had any say about it."

Zach's stiff shoulders and furrowed brow suggested that he was still angry. But it was obvious from seeing Jacob and KC together that they were very much in love. From the sounds of it, they'd overcome a lot to get there.

Sadie knew how Zach felt, though. It was his job to protect his little sister. He hadn't said it outright, but he must feel as though he'd let her down.

The question was, would he understand someone else needing to do the same for their family?

Almost a week later, Sadie stepped into Bella Italia with more trepidation than she'd ever experienced over a formal event. Mostly because she was usually at these things as the help, serving, blending in with the decor rather than standing out like a peacock in a brand-new dress.

She'd known exactly what she wanted to wear when KC had invited her to the Blackstones' party celebrating a new chapter for the mill. The bright blue dress had called to her from the moment she'd walked past the window on the square on the way to Callahan's. Sadie was used to admiring clothes she wasn't able to buy.

Not this time.

For once, she didn't blink at the price. She didn't even use the company card Victor had given her for regular expenses. Somehow that would taint the gift of being invited in the first place. This time she wanted to experience something on her own terms—even if it ended up being a fairy tale.

The sleeveless dress had a fitted bodice that hugged her generous curves and provided ample support. Her second favorite element, besides the color, was a mesh triangle cutout between her breasts, giving a shadowy glimpse of cleavage beneath. The flowy skirt was dressed in sparkles along the calf-length hemline, adding to her festive mood.

She'd indulged in a pair of sexy silver heels without once wondering how many other outfits they would match. Practicality had no place tonight. She wore a single piece of jewelry. The necklace had been a gift from her mother on her twenty-first birthday, the length perfect to nestle a teardrop opal encircled in silver wire in the indention at the base of her throat. A silver shawl completed her dream outfit.

She wasn't sure what had gotten into her, but tonight she would simply go with the flow. Especially since it meant more time with Zachary. A quick look over her shoulder let her watch her prince as he stepped in the door to the restaurant behind her. She'd seen him plenty at the mill in the past few days, but never alone. And there had been no repeat of the night at the B and B.

She wished he had come to get her because he wanted to, not because Christina had asked him to, but the flutters in her stomach were the same, regardless. And the way his dark eyes widened when he saw her in this dress for the first time was very much appreciated.

Zach was a sight to behold himself. The fitted black suit and burgundy tie complemented his dark good looks, making her fingers itch for her camera to record tonight for posterity. She had a small one in her clutch—she was never without one—but wouldn't intrude on a personal gathering by breaking it out.

As Zach took her arm to lead her in, the look on his face was proud—at least, she liked to think so. Even though it didn't dim the wariness that would forever linger in his eyes when he looked at her, still, it made her happy.

This, at least, she could have.

"Well, somebody cleans up good," KC said, giving her brother the once-over before a quick hug.

Zach's gaze flicked to Sadie when she murmured, "I agree."

He wiggled his tie a little to adjust it. "You know I hate these things."

KC shook her head as if she were disappointed in his response. "What's not to enjoy? Great food, friends—even Mom's here." She looked between them, giving Sadie the distinct impression that she was sizing them up together. "Go introduce Sadie, why don't you?"

That definitely started the butterflies in Sadie's stomach. When she'd been here five years ago, she hadn't met any of Zachary's family, though she'd heard a lot about them.

Luckily she had time to compose herself before doing the family thing. She and Zach couldn't get more than a few feet across the floor without someone stopping them to chat. The Blackstones had spared no expense in renting out the entire restaurant for this impressive soiree, and they'd invited all of the upper management from the mill and their families, as well as Zach and KC's family, the mayor and some city officials.

To her surprise, she was almost as much in demand as Zach. The people at the mill and in town had been beyond friendly, and it was no different with tonight's crowd. Sadie felt more at home here than she ever had in Dallas, where she'd lived her entire life. Mostly because the people of Black Hills actually saw her. The real her…or as close to the real her as she could risk showing them.

Suddenly a man with an authoritative bearing appeared at Zach's side, reaching to shake his hand. "I told you this would eventually be cleared up," he said.

"You didn't say it would take this long," Zach answered with a knowing look.

"This is true," the man said with a laugh.

"Sadie," Zach said, pulling her into reach of the conversation, "this is Officer Stephens, my arresting officer."

"What?"

To her consternation, both men chuckled. "Sorry, ma'am," Officer Stephens said. "A little joke. I didn't actually arrest him… I just brought him in for questioning." His wink set her at ease.

"And question me he did," Zach said.

"Just doing my job. But you did good, buddy. Real good."

Zach shook his head. "In the end, it wasn't even me who caught him. It was Luke."

"But you kept pushing," he said, patting Zach's back in that casual way comrades have. "The truth always comes out, my friend."

Sadie forced herself not to shift in her three-inch heels as she heard the words.

"How is Luke?" the officer asked.

"Good." Zach nodded. "He's home, but he opted to stay with Ms. Blackstone tonight. He's had enough of the spotlight for a while."

The officer laughed, shaking his head. "I bet he has."

The men chatted for a minute more before Officer Stephens moved along. Then Sadie turned to Zach. "Luke is the brother who was there when the mill exploded, right?" She'd heard the name all over town, but never met the man himself.

"Yes, Jacob's twin."

As they approached the table where Jacob was solicitously getting KC settled, Sadie studied him. "After seeing the damage, I can't imagine how scary that must have been."

Zach nodded. "They were able to dig him out, along with Mark Zabinski, who set the bomb. They were both injured, though Mark ended up in worse shape than Luke. A wall came down, pinning his legs to the floor."

Sadie winced. "Ouch."

"Ouch, indeed," Zach said as they reached the table.

Not long after everyone was seated and introduced, Aiden and Christina Blackstone also made their way to the table.

"How's Mom?" Sadie heard Jacob ask after giving Christina a quick hug.

"About the same," she replied.

For a moment, Sadie was struck by the silent communication between the Blackstones. Each gaze was tinged with sadness, with a knowledge no one wanted to admit about their beloved mother. But the words weren't spoken aloud. Her own shared glances with her mother were the same. Sadie's heart ached for what the Blackstones were going through; she was going through it with her sister's illness.

From her understanding, Lily Blackstone had been comatose for many years, but in good health… until recently. A series of infections had raised concern for the matriarch. And for Christina, Sadie realized as Aiden pulled his wife close for a moment, resting his palm against her pregnant belly. Sadie was sure the added worry of being Lily's primary nurse did not help in any way.

"What? No camera?" KC asked, distracting Sadie from her sad thoughts.

Sadie lifted her clutch. "In here. I'm rarely without one. Mr. Callahan let me borrow one of his smaller digital cameras, but I didn't want to intrude on a personal gathering. Sometimes people have a hard time enjoying themselves when a camera is in the room."

"What a lovely consideration," Zach's mom said.

"Yes," KC added, "we appreciate the thought, but please feel free. We don't want people to see Black Hills as simply a pile of burning metal and soot." She waved her hand around the room. "Life is a mixture of good and bad, not just the bad. Parties have their place, too."

Sadie signaled her agreement with a smile, but she couldn't help but wonder why everything good in her own life had always led to heartache.

The rich, decadent Italian food only served to make the atmosphere even merrier. Laughter and the scent of tomato sauce mingled in the air. After eating, Sadie excused herself to take a few photographs but seemed to keep Zach in her peripheral vision no matter where she ended up.

He stayed close to his mother, making sure she had everything she needed, though she was far from frail. The family talked easily and continuously, leaving the impression of a perfectly formed group of people that life had brought together. Sadie knew, probably more than most, that it wasn't perfect, though. Zach's father had been a selfish man, leaving Zach's mother with a legacy of heartache and a child to raise alone. The fact that KC's father did the same years later made it that much sadder. And she knew about the Blackstone brothers' sadness over their mother and the danger they had personally faced during the mill's destruction.

But it looked postcard perfect. As did the darkly handsome man in their midst. The man who so easily cared for his family—and possessed the strength and the means to do it.

Unlike Sadie.

Suddenly feeling as if someone had dropped a bag of bricks on her chest, Sadie hurried outside. For long moments she couldn't breathe, couldn't think beyond the need for the cool, fresh air. Ever so slowly, her lungs loosened, letting the air inside, until she no longer felt that her body had seized up. Without thought she drew her phone from her pocket. A quick swipe and she was calling her own mother, almost desperate for the reassurance that she still had some semblance of a family to go home to.

Only no one answered.

There could be a lot of reasons for that. Her mother was in the other room, or tending to Amber. Still, tears welled beneath Sadie's eyelids. She missed her mother so much. And her sister, who was often too weak to talk for more than a few minutes on the phone.

Careful steps took her to the window. She looked in at the party, which was still in full swing. Raising the camera, Sadie took a few shots of the people inside, framed by the decorative greenery on the window casing. She hoped to capture the essence of revelry, especially the family who had so generously offered this opportunity.

But she was on the outside looking in.

And just as Sadie started to feel sorry for herself, Zach turned to face her. His gaze unerringly found her, holding her immobilized with a simple look. A look that laid his soul open, telling her he could be trusted. That a man so beloved by those around him didn't have any dark secrets to hide.

No. The secrets were all hers.

Nine

The minute he'd seen her through the window, he'd known he had to go to her.

Zach wanted to hold her, touch her as he had too few times. But now that he was here, he found himself hesitating. Her beauty in the half darkness, illuminated by the twinkling lights surrounding the window, took his breath away.

She didn't look at him, remaining in profile. "Your family is beautiful," she said.

So are you.

But the yearning in her voice kept him quiet. Somehow he knew, though he could easily seduce her, that this wasn't the time.

"You've built a good life here," she went on. "Are you happy?"

"For the most part," he conceded. Though even surrounded by family and friends he was often lonely, aching. His nature made him a protector, yet he yearned for someone to share the burden with him. "Are you?" he asked, curious.

Sadie had talked very little about her life away from him. Oh, they'd discussed books, music, photography and many other things. But looking back, he realized how little of herself she'd actually given him. As if she were afraid to do so.

"Not often."

In the dim glow he could see her eyes widen; she was surprised by her own response. Why? It was certainly honest. Was she surprised because she'd told him the truth?

And that would be the crux of his wariness when it came to Sadie's return. The more he was with her, the more he was convinced she was holding back, keeping things from him. That wasn't what he wanted. That was why he hadn't gone back to the bed-and-breakfast with her again, even though he wanted more than just one night with her.

So he asked, "What about your family?"

Her hesitation sparked impatience deep inside. "You do have a family, don't you, Sadie?" He took a step closer. "Or are you alone in the world?"

The thought brought sadness for her, tempered

by the knowledge that he could have kept her from being alone…if she had let him.

"Tell me, Sadie." *Something. Anything.*

Then she turned to face him, and his impatience melted away. Tears stood in her eyes like small puddles left from a wintry rain. "I miss my mom," she whispered.

Those gorgeous green eyes slid closed, cutting him off from the aching vulnerability. When they opened again, her gaze was still glassy, but more controlled.

"Where is she?" he asked.

"Dallas." A small smile graced her lips. "I'm not a complete vagabond."

She went quiet once more, a long silence that made him wonder if she would speak again. Just when he gave up hope, she said, "Your mom reminds me of her—hardworking, concerned over her children, never giving up hope." Her deep breath cracked his heart. "I wish I could take care of my mom the way you take care of yours."

"I'm sure she knows that, Sadie." He glanced through the window, seeing people in various groups having a good time. Then he looked at Sadie once more, here on the outside. She wasn't a loner, by any means. He'd seen the way she got along with people, could draw out their stories and make them feel comfortable with her. But yes, she did still keep a part of herself distant.

Just as she did with him.

"If she needs you, why are you here?"

For a moment, he thought she wouldn't answer. Finally she shook her head. "It's the only way I know to help her now."

She didn't elaborate on the cryptic words, so Zach asked, "Your father?"

Sadie shook her head once more. "I don't remember him. He left when I was little. We're a lot alike in that, you and I."

Zach stiffened, bracing himself with one hand against the wall. "How did you know that?" He never talked about his father, preferring not to give attention to someone so utterly lacking in human decency. "You've been snooping around again?"

Her eyes widened, appearing almost scared in the twinkling light. "I wasn't snooping about that. I promise." Her brows drew together. "I can't help it if people like to talk."

"About me?"

"Well, I like talking about you, so why not?" Her lashes lowered over her expressive eyes, as if she knew she'd revealed too much. Suddenly she shivered, drawing the sparkly shawl closer around her shoulders. "Goodness, I didn't realize how cold it had gotten. We should go back inside."

Not yet. As she tried to pass him, Zach reached out. His arms encircled her, his body warming hers in the only way he could in public. Then he leaned down and kissed away the chill.

When he finally pulled back, he felt rather than

saw her grin. "Zachary Gatlin, are you coming on to me?" she asked.

That's what they needed—a little light, a return to the celebration inside. "I don't know—are you willing to risk another interrogation by Miss Gladys?"

He felt her breath catch beneath his palms on her back. "Oh," she whispered. "I think it might be worth it."

As they walked back inside, Zach let his arm remain around her shoulders. Anticipation built, bubbling beneath his skin, only to fizzle out as they rejoined their table. The Blackstone brothers were quietly gathering coats, readying everyone to leave.

"Luke called," Aiden said, turning dark eyes Zach's way. "Mother's temperature has spiked again, but something else is going on. He's concerned. We need to skip out, but I don't want to ruin everyone's evening. Can you take over from here?"

Luckily the mingling of the crowd and the dancing in the back room distracted most everyone from the family's departure. As Zach started making final arrangements, he noticed Sadie falling into organization mode—directing the restaurant staff, taking care of last-minute requests from guests, coordinating cab rides for those who needed them.

Then Zach was left with a final conundrum: the Blackstones' butler and chauffeur, Nolen, had taken them all to Blackstone Manor, where KC and Jacob had a suite with all the baby stuff they needed. That left Zach's mother without a ride home—and her house was in the opposite direction of Sadie's B and B...by quite a distance. While he pondered, Sadie appeared at the table. "It was a pleasure to meet you, Ms. Gatlin," she said, her voice smooth and in control.

Which simply reminded him of just what drove her out of control...

"And you as well, young lady," his mother said. "You handled this party like someone in the know."

"Cleanup is an art form," Sadie said with a slight smile and dismissive wave of her hand. "Just not one normally appreciated by others."

Her words left him to wonder just who she was always cleaning up after.

"Let me just get Mother home, then I'll come by—"

"Nonsense," Sadie said, her eyes overly bright. "The last thing I want to be is trouble. I booked a cab for myself." She patted his arm. He tried not to notice how her touch lingered for a few seconds longer than normal, because it reminded him of an opportunity missed.

"Y'all have a nice night," she said.

Uncomfortable would be more like it.

Sadie told herself she'd come to Lola's because four days was way too long to go without seeing the object of her investigation. Also, a woman had to eat, right?

The impulse had nothing to do with her body's mourning over the lost opportunity or lack of a Zach fix. Not at all. Even though she knew it would have been wrong to accept, she couldn't help but think of his invitation the night of the party with longing. She wished she hadn't given him—and her—the least complicated way out, when her heart had wanted nothing more than to take him home.

The last week had been a busy one for him. The Blackstone brothers had been less hands-on at the mill, splitting their time between there and home with their dying mother. At least that's what gossip around town said: Lily Blackstone's precarious health was finally failing.

The woman's tragic story—of being comatose for many years after a car accident followed by a stroke—left Sadie weepy. She tried not to think about it. Her own sister's terminal illness made the story hit too close to home.

The situation had left Zach with a lot of administrative work on his hands, along with directing his own business. She'd watched at a distance, waiting for the moment when he'd invite her back into the inner circle…but he never did. She told herself he was tired, overworked, but a panic had started deep inside. Yes, she needed to get close to him. She seemed to have found all the superficial evidence about Zach's character she was going to get from the town. Family history, rumors and accusations—none of it would disqualify him from his inheritance. She needed to dig into the parts of his life that no one else could see. In order to find something truly damning, she'd have to find it out from Zach himself.

But the truth was, as wrong as she knew it to be, she wanted that time with him. His attention. His intensity focused on her…for just the few minutes she had left with him.

She'd guessed that he'd be here tonight. He couldn't be spending a lot of time with his family during the day, and family meant a lot to him. That much she'd learned about Zachary Gatlin. So even though he didn't have to work at Lola's, she figured he would be here in some capacity to check on his mother and sister.

The restaurant was full, but not as packed as the last time she'd been here. The scents of grilled meat and some kind of spicy barbecue sauce had her mouth watering in anticipation. She waved to a few friends she'd made as she crossed the floor to nab a small two-top along the wall near the bar, hoping the position would help her see and be seen by one very specific person.

Her disappointment mounted as a waitress took her order and served her food. She'd shared a smile with Ms. Gatlin, Zach's mother, as she busied herself behind the bar. But as dinner wore on, there was no sign of Zach, or even his sister, KC.

As Sadie finished up, the arrival of three women distracted her. They claimed the table directly in Sadie's line of sight near the dance floor. As she looked closer, she noticed that only two of the girls were young, probably early twenties. The other was significantly older. They settled in the chairs and ordered from the waitress.

As soon as she headed back to the kitchen, the older woman smiled at the other two. "You girls head onto the dance floor. It will be a while before the food is here."

They each kissed one of the woman's cheeks, then walked toward the dance floor with eager steps. She smiled after them but didn't look sad to be left behind in the least.

Without warning, her gaze swept over the room before coming to rest on Sadie. They shared a smile.

"Hello, my dear," she said, their tables close enough together that she didn't have to yell, though her voice had certainly not been weakened by age. "Are you dining alone tonight?"

Sadie nodded. "Yes. Just finishing up, actually." She wiped her lips with her napkin, hoping she'd removed any stray barbecue sauce. "Lola's has some of the best food I've found in town."

The woman patted the empty chair next to her. "Indeed they do, which is the excuse I give my granddaughters for bringing me here," she said with a knowing smile. "Join me for a moment. Are you visiting Black Hills?"

"Yes," she confirmed, sliding into the chair. "Thank you, Ms...."

"Saben, dear."

"Ms. Saben. I'm a photographer, working on doc-umenting the rebuilding of the mill."

"Ah, yes. I heard about that. Very exciting."

It certainly had been, but probably not in the way Ms. Saben meant.

"The town—and the Blackstones in particular—have had a very exciting year," she went on. "What with young Aiden coming home and marrying Miss Lily's nurse. Christina is such a lovely young lady."

Ms. Saben smiled at the waitress as she served the drinks. Sadie asked for a refill on her tea and got one. "You doing okay, Miss Saben?" the waitress asked.

"Sure am. Glad to be back in for a bit."

As the waitress went on about her way, Ms. Saben explained, "I've been coming up here for a long time. Ms. Gatlin and I are old friends. But we each have very busy lives." She took a sip of what Sadie had overheard to be a rum and Coke. Ms. Saben tipped the drink in salute. "My granddaughters say it's bad for me to drink, so I've gotta sneak in a little tipple when I can. Otherwise I'd be left watching them down margaritas while I'm drinking water."

Her sass had Sadie laughing out loud.

"Especially now," Ms. Saben went on with a small smile. "I'm just fully recovered from pneumonia. Off all my medicines and pronounced one hundred per-cent by my doctor. If I had to stay in that house one more second, I'd have gone stir-crazy. So I offered to come out here with the girls.

"They get a fun night out from watching me," she

went on. "And I'm not afraid to get out on the dance floor myself in a bit."

"I'll bet you know a thing or two about dancing," Sadie said, inspired by the older woman's daring.

"Honey, you've gotta dance while you still can. Besides, I'd rather break a hip that way than push a walker at the old folks' home."

"Amen," Sadie said with a salute of her tea.

The same muscular server who had delivered Sadie's food earlier came bearing Ms. Saben's potato skin appetizer. Sadie suppressed a grin when the older woman said, "It's a vegetable, right?"

"You got that right, Ms. Saben," the man said before ambling back to the kitchen area.

"I'm so glad Zach was able to hire some decent men to work around here, now that he and KC have so much going on in their lives," Ms. Saben said. "But life does go on, especially new babies." She eyed Sadie. "You have any babies at home?"

"Not yet," Sadie said. Babies were far in her future, if ever. Right now, she had her mom and sister to take care of.

"Well, that little Carter is a joy, and KC deserves her happiness."

"I heard James Blackstone tried to keep KC and Jacob apart…" Sadie prompted, sensing the woman enjoyed telling her stories.

"Indeed he did. And KC had every intention of telling Jacob about the baby, but she was fearful—

for herself and her family. James threatened their livelihood, you know."

"No, I didn't."

"Oh, yes. He owned the land Lola's is built on. Luckily, Jacob and Aiden have deeded it over to KC's mother. You know, so she could feel secure."

Sadie murmured her approval.

"Jacob Blackstone is a good guy. Not like his grandfather. None of the boys are, but there's a lot of men who are none too happy about having the responsibility of a child sprung on them. A lot who would walk away. Ignore it. Not Jacob. And soon there will be a wedding to celebrate, once the, well, sadness is done."

For Lily. They would definitely need some celebration after losing a woman so important to all of them.

As if she were a hunting dog, Sadie suddenly caught the deep timbre of a man's voice and knew immediately that Zach had arrived. Her eyes searched restlessly until she spotted him coming out from the kitchen area, where she knew there was a back entrance.

Apparently Ms. Saben didn't miss her interest. "So that's the way it lies, huh?"

Sadie swung guilty eyes in the older woman's direction. "What?"

"Oh, honey, don't be embarrassed."

Too late. The dreaded heat had bathed Sadie's cheeks already.

"There's not a woman your age who hasn't pined over that one…and a few not your age, too." Ms. Saben giggled like a schoolgirl. "Talk about another good man. One who's had a hard life, but powered through. Nothing like his daddy, either."

And just like that, the seed was planted. There was a theme in both their families' lives—unwanted children. Did Zach have any kids out there he'd neglected? The heart that had yearned for him for five years said he was too responsible for that, too protective. But people were crazy sometimes. Did he have an ex hovering on the fringes, waiting to pounce or holding a child as leverage?

One glance at Ms. Saben told Sadie she had an inkling of the direction of her thoughts, so she might as well be honest. "Does he date a lot?"

Admiration shone in the older woman's gaze. "Honest answer? No. I haven't seen or heard of him dating more than three or four women—why, since he got home from the air force, I guess." She studied Zach as he greeted his mother behind the bar.

So did Sadie. The strong, protective stance drew her, as did the hug he gave his much smaller mother. Her heart instantly melted.

"Maybe that's why…" Ms. Saben mused.

Sadie turned her way. "What?"

Ms. Saben's gaze met hers. "He loves his mama."

Sadie nodded. "And his sister."

Approval lightened the older woman's gaze. "Men who know how to take care of women don't normally play around, because they know how it affects the woman being played with."

Like a ton of bricks, the knowledge hit Sadie. Zach hadn't been playing with her—he wasn't that type of man and didn't have that kind of reputation. And she'd ruined it by walking away...even if she'd done it to protect him.

She couldn't face him with that knowledge so fresh in her heart. Not tonight. Maybe not ever.

Ten

Sadie had been to several impressive mansions throughout her lifetime. Her boss's home was essentially a villa at the end of a lane full of overblown palatial residences that offered every amenity imaginable, including an entire apartment for her in the refurbished barn whose rent came out of Sadie's salary.

But Blackstone Manor gave the impression of a family home despite its grandeur, starting with the red-rimmed eyes of a very fragile-looking butler. "Good afternoon, madam," he said solemnly, prompting an urge to hug him close and comfort him with hot tea.

Neither of which Sadie did, because this wasn't

her home or her rodeo. But her natural sympathy, coupled with the fact that she genuinely liked the Blackstones, made it hard to remain objective.

Lily Blackstone had lingered into January. The family had been able to celebrate Christmas at home, and the announcement of another brother's engagement, without the black cloud of death intruding. That had come with the frigid winds and gray skies of deep winter.

Sadie had been around Black Hills long enough now to give her a tempting feeling of belonging. Some days she wished she could live forever in this sleepy friendly town, with its good, its bad and its quirks.

And except for a brief flight home one weekend to visit her mom, she had.

She and Zach continued to participate in a dance of sorts, a waltz that separated them and brought them close again, but not nearly close enough. Sadie began to recognize that she was procrastinating. She didn't want to have to make a decision, didn't want to figure out what she'd do back home if she didn't get the money to bail her sister out.

At least she was being paid for her current job, even if it meant phone calls from a yelling, screaming Victor almost every night.

Today, she wouldn't think about that. She wouldn't give him the satisfaction of knowing how much he upset her, and she would hold on to the knowledge that his private investigator hadn't had any more luck digging up dirt on Zach than she had.

She greeted Mr. Callahan, Ms. Saben and the Batemans as she made her way across the front parlor. Finally she was beginning to feel welcome. How would she ever live without this when she returned to Texas?

Christina and KC remained at the back of the parlor near the fireplace while many townspeople mingled throughout the room.

"Hello, Sadie," KC said, pulling Sadie into a hug. "We were hoping to get to see you."

"I'm so sorry," Sadie said, feeling the inadequacy of having no true way to comfort them.

"Thank you," Christina replied, ever gracious. "I'm glad you could come by."

Sadie glanced around. "This place is incredible."

KC grinned. "I felt the same way when I first stepped inside. I bet your photographer's senses are at full attention."

"Definitely."

The sound of a large group of people in the foyer had them all turning their heads in that direction. Several couples who had all arrived at the same time made their way to the Blackstone brothers first.

"Looks like we're about to have our hands full," Christina said, patting Sadie's arm. "We'll see you more in a little while, but please feel free to explore."

"And Zach is around here somewhere, too," KC added, her smile looking a little sly to Sadie.

KC hadn't made any secret of her approval as the two women had gotten to know each other more, and had hinted a time or two that she didn't understand why Sadie and Zach didn't at least go on one date. Obviously Zach had not filled his sister in on their history. Sadie wasn't going to do it for him.

It was simply another dark mark on the friendships she was creating here. She told herself she need never see these people again after she betrayed one of their own, which only reinforced the notion that she didn't want to cut them out of her life.

Dangerous thinking.

Sadie wandered around the room, studying the architecture and antiques while she conversed with more of the townspeople. Several of the men she'd gotten to know at the mill introduced her to their families. The Batemans led her across the breezeway into a glorious dining room that had a full spread of food laid out.

They met up with another couple and were distracted talking, so Sadie wandered to the front of the room to look out the window. A man in a dark suit stood to one side of the front windows. He reminded her of other men she'd just passed in the breezeway and front parlor. They were so still they almost faded into the woodwork.

Security.

Then Sadie saw another man approach. She took in the dark tanned skin and close-cropped hair for the first time since she'd returned. He wore a dark suit and tie, along with dark sunglasses to protect his eyes from the winter glare. He paused beside the first man, the angle of his pose allowing her to see the wire for a communication device running up to his ear.

The entire time Sadie had been back in Black Hills, the impact of Zach's new position hadn't really become a reality to her. He'd been directing cleanup and safety crews at the mill. There were other days when she didn't see him at all, and she knew he had taken over an old, established house not far from the town square as his new business headquarters, but she'd never really asked what actually running a security firm entailed.

It made sense that a family who had been targeted for over a year and a half would want this time of grief to be peaceful and safe. They knew the most prominent people in the county, not to mention in the region, and all of the brothers had contacts elsewhere. A lot of people were going to be in and out of this house over the next week.

As he glanced up at the window, it hit home that it was Zach's job to ensure all ran smoothly and safely. Ever the protector. Ever the hero—without all the glory.

Looking at him only brought home just how opposite they were in this situation. He was here to protect those around him. She was here to betray the one they trusted.

Turning, Sadie took her shame with her as she

walked away. Surveying the people mingling and eating in the room, she noticed a small woman at one end of the sideboard picking up a half-empty tray and moving toward a door at the end of the room. Sadie hurried her steps to reach the door just as the woman did.

With a smile Sadie held it open so the woman could slip through unhindered. Sadie herself had performed the maneuver many times, but a helping hand had always been appreciated...and rarely offered.

"Thank you so much, sweetheart," the woman said.

Sadie followed her into a large kitchen filled with the scents of baking. "No problem," she replied, feeling her body relax almost instantly into an environment that held some familiarity for her. Being behind the scenes was much more her forte. "Is there anything I can do to help?"

Stacks of prepared foods in boxes lined several feet of counters. Coolers ran the length of the wall beneath the windows. A glimpse into an open pantry showed shelves lined with dishes and glasses. "Are you doing all of this yourself?" Sadie asked.

"Bless your heart for asking," the woman said, wiping her now empty hands on her apron before extending one toward Sadie. "I'm Marie, the Blackstones' cook and housekeeper." She glanced around at the organized chaos. "And while they know I can work miracles, no, they didn't leave me to do this alone. But the girls who are helping me have taken a quick break."

She shrugged her tiny shoulders, making her Kiss the Cook apron dance. "I thought we would have a bit of a lull, but I was obviously wrong. Normally Nolen would help, but he's got his hands full, too. But those girls have been on their feet all day—they deserve to at least eat lunch sitting down."

"And you don't?" Sadie asked, but she knew exactly how this went. When an event was in full swing, you simply performed the most urgent task, then the next, and the next, until everyone was satisfied. But this event would go on for a few days, which could get grueling.

Reaching for an apron hanging nearby, Sadie draped it over her dark gray dress. "Just point me in the right direction."

They chatted seamlessly for a good twenty minutes as they prepared and replaced platters. Sadie brushed aside Marie's protests as she loaded the dishwasher. It needed doing, so she did it.

Until a six-foot-two hunk of dark charisma walked through the doorway. Sadie couldn't help it—her every motion stopped, including her breath. Not too long, but long enough for Marie to notice.

Long enough to earn her a knowing grin from the older woman.

"So you're still here," Zach said.

If she hadn't been glancing in his direction, Sadie

wouldn't have known he was speaking to her. She straightened. "Where else would I be?"

"When you disappeared, I assumed you went home without at least saying hi."

Her heartbeat resumed, a little faster this time. For a moment, she'd thought he meant here as in Black Hills, not here as in Blackstone Manor. "No, I'm just trying to lend a hand."

His dark gaze slid over to Marie. "She's good at that, isn't she?"

"Most definitely."

He approached the older woman and folded her carefully into his arms, as if she were too fragile to be in charge of an army's worth of food. "I'm sorry, Marie."

Tears prickled behind Sadie's eyes as the older woman seemed to melt into him. She'd given Sadie, and probably everyone else, the impression that she was coping just fine, thank you very much. But one hug and the facade shattered. She didn't cry, but the pain showed on her aging face nonetheless.

"I'd been with her since she was a baby," Marie said.

"I know," Zach murmured, so tender Sadie had to look away.

"The car accident was hard," Marie went on. "But she was still here, still with us. Then the stroke… she's really been gone since then, but it wasn't real, you know."

The words struck Sadie's heart unexpectedly.

There were times when her sister got so sick that she disappeared into unconsciousness for days. One time the doctors had to put her in a medically induced coma. But she always came back...there was always hope. Lily Blackstone had had none.

A rustle of fabric drew Sadie's gaze once more. Marie had straightened and was smoothing down her apron. "I wish she could have been here to see all the boys come home." She smiled at Zach, though it was a little shaky around the edges. "Your sister. Carter. This new young'un on the way. She would have loved all of it."

Life. It had been all around Lily, but she'd been unaware. Amber was the same, in certain ways. Her life was a series of doctor visits, debilitating treatments, recuperating and quiet nights at home with her mom and sister.

How much longer before she had no life at all? The weight of the thought sat on Sadie's chest, constricting her breath.

"Yes, she would have," Zach said. "She created a beautiful family."

"A legacy," Marie agreed.

And Amber would have none.

Suddenly the walls wavered. Sadie knew if she didn't get out of there, she was going to embarrass herself by either weeping copiously or passing out. Neither option made her very happy.

Her throat was too constricted to speak, to excuse herself. She lurched for the back door, stumbled through a closed-in porch, then burst into the weak sunshine. Not sure why, she kept moving forward, as if the motion would somehow jump-start her body into behaving again. But suddenly she was halted by a set of heavy hands on her shoulders.

Her body was pulled upright, then back against a solid, muscular chest. The warmth soothed her, making her aware that she was out in the cool January air with no coat over her dress. Just an apron. The thought made her want to laugh, but her lungs were strained.

Zach leaned in close, burying his face against her neck. His heat surrounded her. "Just breathe, baby," he murmured against her ear.

Zach felt Sadie's body unlock as if he'd turned the key. Breathing deep, she rose up on her toes. Then she collapsed back against him.

Leaving him feeling like he'd won the lottery.

He sensed her beginning to relax. The feel of her ribs expanding beneath his palms. The loosening of her muscles against his chest. The sigh that finally graced his ears.

He waited for her to sag as the tension drained from her, but Sadie was too strong for that. Instead her knees locked. She didn't pull away, but she wasn't relying solely on him for her stability, either.

That was the essence of the woman he'd come to know.

And she was kind, compassionate, hardworking. Today, he was determined to learn something new.

Stepping back was a hardship, but he substituted holding her hand for the embrace. A poor substitute, his body said. He led her to a bench near this end of the sloping back lawn. During the summer, irises bloomed plentifully here, but the now-barren leaves didn't detract from the richness of the view.

He took a quick inventory of her. Breath steady. Eyes closed. Pulse slowing beneath his palm. He waited a few minutes more before pushing.

"Tell me what that was about."

"A panic attack," she said simply. "I've had a few over the years, but they're so rare that I never feel quite prepared for them."

Her deep breath drew his gaze down to the fullness of her chest, even though he knew that's not where his focus should be right now.

"Marie's words...they just brought up some bad memories for me."

"Did you lose someone you love?"

She shook her head, but it wasn't really an answer—more the movement of someone trying to deny reality. "Not yet...but I will."

He waited, trying to wrap his mind around her words. Was it her mother? That was the only relative she'd ever mentioned.

"I have a sister...a baby sister."

Zach felt his world tilt slightly, then right itself.

"She was diagnosed when she was a teenager. The

cancer is terminal at this point." A sad smile tilted the corners of her lips. "She's a trouper—it's been six years since her diagnosis. They said she would only live two."

Zach could read between the lines. "But she won't be able to fight it forever?"

Sadie shook her head, her lips pressed tight for control. Fortunately, he could read all her emotions in those expressive eyes.

"No," she finally conceded. "She's fought long and hard, but her resolve is weakening. As is ours— mine and my mother's. We take the best care of her we can, but there's only so much we can do."

"And that's heartbreaking."

"My poor mother—she's handled the majority of Amber's care, but it's too much. We had to place her in a type of halfway house. Not hospice…yet." Sadie looked away, but Zach could still see her neck working as she swallowed.

As he'd done with Marie, he reached out to comfort her. Only this wasn't Marie. He reacted in a completely different manner that shook him deep inside. But he didn't let go.

"I was still young myself, but about a year into her treatment I took over my mother's position as housekeeper for our former employer so she could stay home with Amber full-time. This trip is the longest I've been away from them, ever."

In her voice, Zach heard an echo of his own struggles with responsibility. The burden of doing whatever you had to in order to care for someone you love, regardless of where you wanted your own life to go. It was a heavy weight, one he hated to think of on Sadie's slim shoulders. But it came with its own rewards.

He was sure she knew that by now also.

"Why did you leave now, Sadie?"

She went still beneath his touch, and for a moment he worried that his question had seemed judgmental. But Zach was the last one to judge. He'd left his entire family behind for the military because that's what he'd needed to do to provide a better life for them.

"The trip—it was a legacy, of sorts, from our former employer," she said. "The chance to travel outside our little world. My mom wouldn't hear of me giving it up—neither of them would."

He knew he shouldn't ask, but he couldn't stop himself. "So you could go anywhere, and you chose to come here."

She quickly glanced at him out of the corner of her eye, which told him she realized the significance of the question. "Zach, this is the only place I wanted to be." She wiped shaky fingers over her cheeks. "I'm sorry. This is just a little too close," she whispered.

For a moment, he thought she meant him. But now she clutched his arms, her body leaning into his. Then he understood. Marie had been talking about life, the life Lily should have had.

The life Amber should have had.

"I know it is," he said. "And that's okay."

With a jerk her gaze swung up to meet his. He could read the conflict in her eyes. The woman she'd shown him was strong, independent, but soft with others. Now she needed to take care of herself.

"It's okay, Sadie. Feeling that way doesn't make you weak. It makes you human."

That's when the tears appeared, just like the night she'd told him she missed her mother. They pooled like shiny puddles in her eyes, reflecting that incredible green color. He knew then, no matter what he really wanted, he would never be able to get over Sadie.

Whether she stayed or not.

Eleven

When her phone rang, Sadie was surprised to see Zach's name lighting up the small screen. But her hesitation lasted only a second before she answered.

"Pack a weekend bag and meet me downstairs."

She opened her mouth to reply, but the line went dead. Was he already downstairs? Should she go question him? Why was she even thinking about this?

Letting go of her worrisome thoughts, she packed her travel toiletries and enough clothes for two days into an oversize purse in record time. The sound of her feet on the stairs as she descended ramped up her heartbeat.

It had only been a day and a half since she'd seen him, but it seemed like forever. She'd chosen not to attend Lily Blackstone's funeral today, figuring she'd simply be lost in the throng of people who would be there. But Zach had surely braved the crowds for the family who had done so much for him.

When he'd last said goodbye at Blackstone Manor, he'd told her he would be in touch, but not when. That made sense, considering his position as head of security for the family. She definitely hadn't expected to speak with him tonight after what had undoubtedly been a long day.

Shouldn't he be home relaxing? Sleeping?

Yet there he stood in the foyer of the B and B, looking a little tired around the edges, but fresh in a pair of jeans and a T-shirt. She wished she could run her fingers through his hair or savor the sexiness of his gaze as he did a little inspecting of his own.

But he didn't linger. He quickly took her bag and led her out to a low, dark sports car. Still without an explanation, he seated her in the front, then stowed her bag in the trunk. Her first clue as to his intentions was his quick lean across the seat after he climbed behind the steering wheel. His lips on hers were hot and hard, telling her without words of the need he barely held in check.

Her anticipation exploded into full-blown excitement.

Good thing he wasn't dangerous, because she had no recollection of where they drove. Her entire focus was on the smallest of things: his hands on the steering wheel, the barest hint of music on the radio—too low for her to tell what it was—the shaking in her core that had nothing to do with fear and everything to do with Zach.

It wasn't until he pulled the car into an almost empty lot and parked that reality hit. She realized she needed to know. "Zach," she stalled, before he could open his door.

"Yes?"

His low voice only sent further shivers up her spine. "I'm guessing we're not going out to dinner?" She tried to keep her tone light, but Zach plunged straight into the deep end.

He leaned closer, invading her comfort zone. "We both know what's happening, Sadie. I think it's time to stop beating around the bush, don't you?"

"Um…"

"Don't pretend this isn't what you want." If his words didn't convince her, the way his lips traced her jaw definitely did.

But for once, she needed honesty between them. "I won't." Heaven knew she couldn't. "But how can it be what you want?" She swallowed hard but forced herself to finish. "After I left?"

"You were trying to do the right thing, weren't you?"

He would never know it, but she had. Her attempt to protect him from the callous, self-centered man who had been his father might not be the right thing in his mind, but it had been in hers. "Yes."

"That's the most important thing to me, Sadie."

She instantly cooled as he got out of the car and walked around to her side. If she hadn't known she would ultimately lose Zach, those words had spelled it out loud and clear. But she didn't have time to contemplate. Zach opened her door. His hand folded over hers, and he eased her out onto her feet. "I want you," he said, no longer holding back. "You have responsibilities away from here. I totally understand that."

He lifted her chin with his other hand, positioning her lips exactly right for his kiss. "If I only have you for this weekend, so be it."

Her defenses and resistance fell with his words, and she had a feeling she'd never be able to rebuild either again. Instead she took a deep breath and nodded. "Okay." Her voice wasn't too shaky, at least.

As he locked up the car, she glanced around. Parts of Black Hills had become fairly familiar to her by now, but she had absolutely no idea where she was at the moment. Zach grabbed their bags, then her hand and led her across the asphalt to a large metal building.

They were spending the weekend in a manufacturing plant? It certainly didn't have the romantic feel she would expect, but then, Zach was a guy. The dark night kept her from reading the sign farther down the wall. It wasn't until they passed through the double doors that Sadie got a clue.

They'd arrived at the small municipal airport. The too bright, fluorescent-lit space wasn't big enough for commercial traffic—mostly crop dusters and shuttle planes. Which also explained why it was mostly deserted at this time of the evening.

Zach dumped their bags near a grouping of chairs and waved her into a seat. "I'll just get everything set up."

Sure he would. She remembered him talking about loving every minute of learning to fly in the military, and he'd done some crop dusting in town until the notorious cotton killings last year.

"Zach, would you mind telling me what we're doing?"

He paused a few feet away, his expression filled with an almost childlike excitement. "Do you like surprises?"

A frown started between her brows. "I haven't had any good ones in my life."

"Well, let's try this one and see."

Zach felt like he'd spent the entire two-hour flight grinning—and he wasn't a grin type of guy. He preferred a smirk or a glare. But the reaction to Sadie's every gasp and sigh was unstoppable.

Despite her initial shock, it was clear she'd enjoyed the view, no matter their altitude. Zach's new private plane, no matter that it was small, made the trip pure pleasure. It was the first thing he'd bought for himself since he'd hit the big time. Add on the anticipation of being with Sadie, and yeah, he grinned.

He was giving himself a gift, and hopefully giving her one, too. He'd told her the truth: the past was the past. He didn't need a crystal ball to guess the future was uncertain. But for this weekend, they would have all they wanted of each other.

No more interruptions.

He took the plane down and handled the technicalities at the airport with ease but not nearly enough speed for his liking. It took way too long to get everything loaded into the Jeep he kept at the airport and get started on the road.

"We'll be at our destination in about twenty minutes," he said.

At least, he hoped so. He hadn't checked the weather forecast the way he normally did before his trips, and a light snow had started to fall as they ascended the mountain.

"Where are we going?" she asked.

"My favorite place in the world."

She didn't question him further but grinned herself. Then she turned her gaze back out the window to the darkened landscape. "Well, I already know it's beautiful," she said in a hushed voice.

As did he. The real estate agent was the most trusted in Black Hills, a woman Zach had known most of his adult life. He'd laid out his specifications, and in a week she had an even dozen options from a trusted network of agents all over the South. This one had stood out from the rest at first glance. He'd made the purchase without hesitation—and without familial consent. Heck, his family didn't even know the specifics about this place. And they'd never actually been here.

He came to the cabin regularly. Always alone. It was the one place he could let down his guard, let go of the ever-present responsibility and truly relax. He'd never wanted anyone else's personality to imprint on the place…until now.

Maybe he should have planned this a little more, but Zach knew all about trusting his instincts. The impulse was true. At least when Sadie was gone, he'd be able to come here and remember her.

Even he had to admit that the cabin looked charming as they arrived. The light, fluffy snow had started to accumulate on the nooks and crannies of the log house and roof. He parked out in front instead of pulling in close. The cabin wasn't large, though it did have two bedrooms and two baths. The second story held only the master bedroom, bath and sitting area.

Not big, but it had all the amenities he'd wanted. A wide wraparound porch perfect for relaxing. A balcony with a hot tub, accessible from the master suite. An environmentally friendly exterior finish. And the whole thing was surrounded on three sides by a forest dense with cedar and pine.

"Wow, Zach. This is gorgeous."

He helped Sadie out of the Jeep and grabbed both of their bags before leading her up the stairs to the porch. Her red hair glinted with snowflakes, tempting him to keep her outside to admire her beauty. But his body protested any further delay.

The security system and locks were a minute's work for him. Then they were stepping through the door into the slightly cool interior. Dropping the bags, he made a beeline for the opposite wall and adjusted the thermostat.

"I keep it cooler in here when I'm away—just high enough to keep everything from freezing—but it will warm up soon."

She nodded, her eyes twinkling with excitement as she surveyed the interior. "I'm serious, Zach. This has to be your best-kept secret. I love it."

Arms tucked around her to combat the chill, she wandered through the downstairs area. But her words held him still. Because the cabin was a secret of sorts. He never talked about it with anyone; he'd never even described it or shown his family any pictures, even though they knew of its existence.

Because deep down, he felt guilty for taking this time, this space for himself.

The admission stunned him. Guilt was a weakness he couldn't afford and didn't have the time to wallow in.

Suddenly Sadie stood before him, her appearance shaking him from his daze. "You're right," he told her, "it is my secret. You're the only person I've ever brought here."

Her green eyes widened. He could almost see the impact as his confession hit her. Then she narrowed her gaze on him. "Why, Zach?" she asked, soft-spoken but demanding in her own way. "Why wouldn't you want people to know about this part of your life?"

"They wouldn't understand why I want to be here…need to be here." The explanation burned in his throat.

Sadie reached out to him, offering comfort instead of the passion he'd planned on when he'd first walked through the door. "I understand. Sometimes life is overwhelming, and you need to recharge—somewhere away from all the things you feel like you have to take care of."

She stepped in close, the arm around his waist making him wish there was nothing between his skin and hers. "You've worked incredibly hard, Zach. You deserve this sanctuary for yourself."

"Sometimes it doesn't feel like it."

"Why?"

He shook his head. "If it wasn't for the Blackstone brothers, I'd probably be rotting in jail from that crop dusting incident. To have everyone patting my back…it just feels false."

Sadie wasn't buying it. "You've worked at the mill a long time, right? Long before you were head of security for the Blackstones."

Zach nodded.

"You've known most of those people all of your life, right?"

"Yes."

"I saw you with them, Zach," she said, squeezing him a little tighter. "I've watched you interact with them since that first trip out there. They respect you. Your direction and judgment."

Her gaze remained clear and direct, pulling him in.

"That doesn't come from Blackstone backing. You have to earn that. Which you did with your integrity and hard work. They know you because you've proven yourself time and again. And that's why they won't judge you for indulging in some of what we girls call me time every so often."

Her assessment left him speechless and in desperate need of a few minutes to himself. As if she completely understood, she graced him with a sweet smile and continued on her exploration.

Leaving him and his emotions behind.

Twelve

Eager for something to do, Zach carried the bags up the stairs to the master suite. Simply furnished in beige suede with accents reminiscent of the nearby woods, the atmosphere was soothing without being feminine. He dropped the bags, wondering where he would put Sadie's stuff.

With a self-deprecating shake of his head, he conceded that he hadn't thought through his plans for this visit very well. He could put her bag downstairs, but he wasn't about to give even a ghost of an impression that he wanted her that far away. Upstairs, he had a few drawers built into the closet, filled with his own clothes.

Maybe they'd stay busy enough that clothes wouldn't be necessary.

They definitely weren't necessary for what he had in mind. He glanced from the bed to the French doors leading to the balcony and hot tub. For the first time, Zach planned to explore every fantasy he could with a woman. Until now, he'd always held back. The intensity of his nature kept him cautious.

But tonight he was cutting the caution tape and diving in headfirst.

As he heard her footsteps on the stairs, a tremble started in his hands. Not hard enough to be seen, just subtle enough to be felt. He clenched his fists, unwilling to give in to the need to pounce the minute she strolled through the doorway.

But when she came in, she didn't look around, didn't inspect her surroundings with the curiosity she had downstairs. Instead her gaze rested solely on him.

Just as she had downstairs, she reached for him. Only this time, her touch wasn't intended for comfort. She moved in close. The faint scent of sugar drifted over him as her hands traveled across his chest to grasp the edges of his open flannel shirt. Slowly she pulled down, just hard enough for him to feel the weight. Then she let go and slipped her hands inside. The same feeling of need came over him, multiplied by a hundred.

But he refused to take the reins...just yet.

The light scrape of her nails against his ribs

through the undershirt tested his resolve. His eyelids slid closed. A few deep breaths might help…

She pressed her mouth against the underside of his jaw.

…maybe not.

His heart raced as she nibbled and licked her way to his neck, then down along the sensitive skin of his throat. He growled a warning.

And heard her giggle.

With a quick move, he lifted her by her arms and tossed her lightly onto the bed behind them. A high-pitched squeal signaled her surprise. He stood his ground at the mattress's edge, staring down at her with the knowledge that the game was now his. He was in control. He would make the next move.

For both their pleasure.

"Strip."

The command sounded loud in the room, firm in its intent. Her eyes widened, and he didn't miss the catch in her breath. Slowly, as if to tease him, she crawled to her knees, then straightened. Her fingers traced up her sweater to the trio of buttons right below her breasts. He could almost feel the seconds tick out as she released each one with agonizing delays.

If she only knew just where that teasing would lead.

Next came the long-sleeved T-shirt beneath. How could a woman make pulling a shirt over her head so incredibly sensual? As she reached for the button of her jeans, the tremble in his hands became a reality.

The zipper traveled down ever so slowly. Just when he wondered how she would complete the move, she rolled confidently down onto her back. Holding his gaze with her own, she braced her knees and lifted her hips into his line of sight. She worked the heavy material down over her hips, then paused with her palms flat against her thighs.

Now it was his turn.

His patience at an end, he grasped the material and pulled. The jeans came off in one easy move. Sadie lost her balance as her feet were swept off the bed and fell back with a little bounce. The lamp on the bedside table left no shadows to hide her body. Zach was free to savor every inch with his gaze as much as his touch.

He took advantage as he systematically stripped his own clothes away. As he crawled onto the bed, a new feeling took hold of him. He didn't recognize it at first. When he did, he probably should have been ashamed. After all, this was the age when women weren't owned by men. But deep inside, the urge to brand her as his was undeniable. To cover her body with his own and take her until no other man would dare touch what was Zach's alone.

Primitive. Forceful. Necessary.

He could concede that this relationship wasn't forever as long as he wanted to…but his body would never believe it.

Straddling her stomach and arms, he bent low over her upper body. Just as she had earlier, he pressed kisses along her lower jaw. Only his were openmouthed and hard, drawing moans from deep within her throat. He moved lower, sucking at the base of her neck where the delicate indentation between her collarbones begged for his attention.

She squirmed, but he wasn't giving her the chance to distract him with her touch. As he traveled out to the delicate structure of her shoulder, he swept the strap of her bra aside. Then he stripped the bra itself down to reveal pale, trembling mounds of succulent flesh. Pressing them together with his palms, Zach admired their strawberries-and-cream color before lowering his head to drive her wild.

Because he remembered everything that made Sadie moan, sigh and cry out. And he used that knowledge to his full advantage.

As much as he wanted to hold out, to extend their loving to the brink of insanity, the throbbing pulse between his thighs insisted otherwise. He made quick work of her undergarments, then took immense satisfaction in lifting her legs and wrapping them around his waist.

She needed no prompting but immediately pulled him in tight. He barely had enough reach to snag a condom from the bedside table and cover himself. Then he slid home.

This time, there was no controlling his rhythm, no holding back. Their bodies strained in time with each other. Her cries filled the air. The feel of her fingernails on his back sent a sharp zing down his spine.

Almost over. Not yet. *Not yet.*

He buried his face at her throat, absorbing the vibration of her hoarse cries with his mouth. Her body tightened around him, a long, slow squeeze that pulled him in and sucked him dry.

It was many moments before Zach could open his eyes to the glare of the lamp beside them, even more before he could ease away from the tangle of their limbs. He made them both comfortable, then plunged the room into darkness.

A dim glow from outside permeated the French doors. Not the light of the moon, but maybe its shadowy reflection off the ever deepening snow on the deck. He lay on his side watching it, Sadie pulled close and secure against his chest. As he listened to the deepening of her breath, he had the same feeling he'd had on the nights before a few missions gone wrong. The sense that he'd made a mistake, missed something that was going to come back to bite him in the ass.

But he was too happy to care. If Sadie was a mistake, she was by far the best mistake he'd ever made.

"But I didn't bring a swimsuit."

The amused, calculating look in Zach's eyes told her he didn't care. Not in the least. "Well, I have one, but I promise not to use it."

Oh, she was in trouble. But she tried to protest

anyway. "It's cold out there." The idea of the hot tub in the snow sounded romantic, but she'd have to actually go outside naked to accomplish it.

"So…"

As Zach tracked her around the bedroom, Sadie tried to think of another motive for staying inside. Normally, dawn was something she only saw for photo shoots. But this seemed to be her punishment for trying to ease out of bed and find a robe to cover her naked body. Now she attempted to both avoid Zach and keep the robe, which proved useless as he pounced.

Her squeal echoed in the room when he swept her into his arms and stalked for the French doors. The first blast of cold air on her bare bottom made her gasp.

Yep, exactly what she had wanted to avoid.

The Neanderthal carrying her didn't appear fazed. "Zach," she said. "I'm naked."

"And all the more beautiful for it."

Thankfully Zach had prepared the tub while she'd been in the bathroom. The cover was already off and steam rose in smoky tendrils from the water. After a few steps, he tilted her until her toes met the blessed warmth. Inch by inch he eased her in until the water covered her like a blanket. Then he slid his sleekly muscled limbs in behind her.

The water bubbled against her skin, reawakening the sensual needs that simmered below the surface whenever Zach was anywhere close. Zach's strong hands kneaded her shoulders, further weakening her resistance.

"See," he murmured. "This is worth the walk, right? Or rather, the ride?"

"Totally," she mumbled back. "And I'll believe that until the minute I have to get out and walk back into the house."

Zach laughed, the sound echoing around them. "Then I better make the interim worthwhile, huh?"

You always do.

But she didn't let herself say the words out loud. She let her body speak them instead.

It wasn't long before Zach's hands moved from working their heavenly magic on her shoulders back up into the wildly tangled locks of her hair. He alternated hands, squeezing and pulling one at a time, just enough to release the tension from her scalp.

Sadie thought she might melt into eternal bliss.

Every touch, every word spoken became a treasure to hide in her heart. The only gift she might ever be able to give herself, because once she had to leave him, nothing else would ever compare to these memories.

Suddenly his hand in her hair was guiding her. A nearby seat hidden in the bubbles became a shelf for her to brace against. The vista before her swirled with dancing snow swept up from the forest floor, and the saturated pinks and blues of sunrise reflected off sparkling icicles.

She felt Zach's warm skin against her back, forming a shield between her and the cool air. Not that she noticed. Her mind was too focused on the moment when he made them one, bringing their bodies together in a connection as glorious as the beauty around them.

He moved inside her, all around her. The water splashed and bubbled in an accompaniment to their harsh breath. His fingers continued their ballet of tightening and letting go, building her anticipation.

"You're so beautiful, Sadie," he murmured with his mouth against her shoulder, only adding to the myriad sensations.

How could she ever let go of such perfection?

In response to the thought, her body clamped down, desperate to hold him within her for as long as she could. She arched her back, trying to take him deeper. To make him as much a part of her as she could.

He moved in and out, every drag and pull intensifying her response. The low rumble of his voice added to the tingles, coaxing her into submission, commanding her response. Finally, just as the sun peeked over the horizon, her orgasm rolled through her, forcing Zach to catch his breath. He held still, buried in her inch by glorious inch.

Her mind exploded along with her body, screaming the knowledge of her love for this man. So loud, she had to bite down on her tongue to hold the words inside. Instead tears fell, mingling with the steam surrounding them.

Zach groaned, thrusting a few last times before he slowed down with a sigh. He pressed firm kisses along her shoulder as his arms surrounding her trembled ever so slightly. He murmured tender, soothing words against her skin.

Something inside Sadie died at the thought that she couldn't have him forever. But as her eyes drifted closed, she did her best to imprint every second to memory.

Then again, how could she ever forget any of these incredible moments? She only hoped she never did.

There was a lot to be learned about another person when you spent several days in a row alone together, just as Sadie did during their time snowed in at the cabin. Sharing the same bed brought a whole wealth of knowledge.

And not just about sex.

For instance, Zach was a side sleeper. He cuddled in close every night, but her position didn't seem to matter. She could face out spoon style, or snuggle her cheek against his chest. Either way, he almost never moved more than the barest shift. He wasn't a tosser and turner, which made sleeping with him a bit like having access to her own human pillow that supported her body and didn't self-adjust after she'd made herself comfortable.

It might have sounded uptight, but Sadie had learned after many interrupted nights' sleep with her sister that she could only be awakened so many times before her brain started to short-circuit. Sleep was, quite frankly, important to her.

Tonight, their third here, started the same as both the other nights. Sadie drifted off to sleep wondering how many more nights she would have like this. Would they be going home tomorrow? Were the roads safe up here? She hadn't had more than the briefest of glimpses out at the road and wasn't sure that she wanted one.

Frankly, she didn't want their time together to end.

An adulthood spent in a sickroom had given her the unfortunate ability to instantly wake up at the slightest noise or movement. Only Zach's movements weren't slight.

First he flopped onto his back so that his side bumped against her back. She rolled over to face him then snuggled up to a pillow instead. He was probably trying to get comfortable. Then he jerked again, mumbling something under his breath.

A little odd for the man who usually slept like a rock for six hours a night. Reaching out, she laid her palm against his bare chest. His skin was hot, with a light sheen of sweat.

A few seconds later, he jolted again. Then again, and again. It took her a few minutes to realize that the man she thought couldn't be shaken was having a nightmare. Seconds later he rolled over, this time throwing out an arm that caught her unawares as it struck against her side.

Her gasp sounded loud in the room. Suddenly,

Zach sat straight up, his body at attention. Sadie froze, too, not sure whether or not it was safe to reach out again. Who knew what Zach was reacting to—and she had a feeling he wasn't entirely awake.

So she held still, counting the spaces between his breaths, waiting for him to gain consciousness. As he did, the feel of the room changed. His muscles loosened one by one. Then the sound of a ragged breath met her ears, interrupted by a hard swallow.

When he turned to her, she couldn't see his expression in the gloom, but she could hear the emotion in his voice. "Sadie? Sadie, are you okay?"

Now she sat up, automatically reaching out a hand to rest against his biceps. "I'm okay, Zach."

She barely made out the shadow of him shaking his head. "I think—I think I hit you." His ragged breathing continued. "I'm damn sorry, Sadie."

"I'm perfectly fine," she assured him. "It was more like a bump. I was just in the way, Zach. No harm done."

"I still shouldn't have…"

That's when she realized there was a slight tremble beneath her palm. Not a full-blown reaction. Something she suspected he was using all his might to control. But it was there, all the same.

"That must have been a doozy of a nightmare," she said.

Even Sadie, who kept a lot to herself, would have wanted to talk something like that out. If for no other reason than to rid herself of the haunting images that could linger after a very intense nightmare.

Apparently Zach didn't, because he was silent. Which was fine. It wasn't for her to decide what Zach wanted to share. But that didn't stop her protective instincts from surging to the front.

Being protected, being taken care of, was as foreign to Zach as it was to Sadie. She wasn't going to let that hold her back.

Curling her fingers around his elbow, she pulled him in her direction. He resisted at first, but she wasn't giving up. As he twisted toward her, she reached for his other arm, then used them to guide him down against her. She lay back against her pillow, positioning him along her side.

"It's okay, Zach," she repeated softly.

Her heart leaped as he buried his face against her neck, but she held still. It took time. Soon his skin was flush against hers, his breath puffing gently along her collarbone and his arm heavy across her waist. There were no more signs of the shakes, but she sensed a struggle for balance. One she couldn't influence, but she could provide a safe haven until he found it.

She embraced his shoulders, securing him to her. Then she closed her eyes and measured her breaths. Soon his breathing matched hers, his rhythm evening out. Only then could she truly relax deep down inside, no longer worried that the nightmare would win.

He might not sleep well, but at least his body could rest.

But sleeping didn't seem to be what he had in mind. Just as she began drifting toward slumber, his leg shifted over hers, sliding between her thighs. Languidly his hand explored what flesh it could find.

And she was more than happy to welcome his touch.

She kept waiting for him to speed up, to channel the adrenaline from his dream into a headlong rush for oblivion. Instead, he seemed to lose himself in pleasuring her, drawing out every caress to gift her with the ultimate in sensation.

Sadie found herself drowning in the unexpected sensuality that lasted longer than she could have dreamed possible, until every inch of her body was imprinted with the memory of Zach on a cellular level that meant he would be with her forever.

She still wasn't sure if a forever without him was something she could survive.

Thirteen

Zach let Sadie sleep.

It was the least he could do after waking her up last night. The thought that he could have hurt her during his dream hung like a chain around his neck.

Something he wasn't proud of.

But he'd survive. He'd learned long ago that he could do this. He would do this. Healing just took time.

As did other things.

He remembered staring down at Sadie's back as he made love to her in the hot tub. The flex and pull of her muscles fascinated him, because they represented the strength and character of a woman who worked hard and provided for others when she could. A woman he loved.

If he'd had any doubts before now, they'd been obliterated last night. But emotions were much easier to face and acknowledge in the dark of night. Now he was about to face her across the breakfast table, and he had some explaining to do...

Which always went down better with food. His mama had taught him that.

He was in the middle of cooking up waffles, scrambled eggs and bacon from the supplies his caretaker had brought in when Sadie made her way into the kitchen. The sexy tumble of her hair made him think of all the things he'd done to her during the night. His body's elation muted the slight panic over his plan for this morning.

Her gaze followed him as he moved, but she didn't ask any questions. He could go with it and not bring up the nightmare he'd suffered for the first time in a year or more, keeping his secrets to himself. He hadn't even fully shared the experience that caused the nightmares with his family.

But he saw that as the dipwad way of handling this. He wasn't going to take the easy way out—that wasn't the kind of man he was.

"Are you trying to butter me up?" she asked, peering over his shoulder. "Because waffles are definitely the way to go."

He'd noticed her love of both waffles and pancakes whenever Gladys served them at the B and B. So he might have been working with a little insider knowledge.

"Do I need to?" he asked, glancing at her over his shoulder as he plated the food.

Sadie didn't look away or back down. Her gaze held his. "Absolutely not."

Good to know. He hadn't hurt her when he was thrashing around last night. She'd told the truth—she was fine. Now he would do the same.

He let her dig in first, lifting forkfuls of buttery, syrupy goodness to her lips before he got down to the dirty details.

"A lot happens in the years you serve your country," he started. "Some of it is good—very good. Like the men and women you serve with. They become like a second family."

He chewed thoughtfully on a piece of bacon. Sadie had slowed her own bites, as if her initial hunger had been eased somewhat.

"Some of it is bad—very bad."

"I'm sure." Her soothing voice coated his nerves like a balm. It was the very thing that had drawn him to her five years ago, that voice.

"One particular day was beyond bad." He blinked, questioning for a moment whether he could actually do this. With a deep breath, he forced himself to continue. "I thought we were all gonna die. My platoon. My brothers." Without warning his throat tightened, closing off his voice, his breath. The memory of that day could still tear him up even now. "But a friend, my best friend, actually, saved us all by throwing himself over an IED."

Unable to handle whatever sympathy he might see in her face, he stared down at his plate. "He died instantly."

Abstractly, he noticed the tight grip his fingers now had on his fork and forced them to loosen one by one. This mere exercise in concentration helped get him back on track.

"The nightmare is always the same," he said. "I go back through the entire day, but I'm only observing it. I can't stop anything from happening. I see all of the things I missed, everything I could have done to stop it."

He clenched and unclenched his fists. "I yell at myself until I'm hoarse, but it does no good. I watch helplessly, unable to prevent his death like I should."

Her gentle voice intervened. "Why should you?"

"It's my job," he said, handing over the rote answer, the least complicated one.

"You're right," she answered. "You are responsible."

That had him looking up, misery snaking through his heart. But she reached out to cover his hand with her own. "Because you've made yourself responsible. But your friend would not want you to spend your life beating yourself up.

"Just like my sister doesn't want me to stay home—" she pulled back from him "—to stop living, just for her. Their wishes don't ease the sense of obligation or guilt, but ultimately, they want us to live, even though they can't."

Sadie dropped her fork onto her plate. He thought about her sister and how hard it must have been for her to encourage Sadie to leave her. He thought about his own mother and the many times she'd told him to go out and have fun.

Yet the only way he could do that was at an isolated cabin in the woods, because everywhere else he went there were things to do and people to take care of.

"Is that why you left the military?" Sadie asked.

Zach sat for long moments, unable to answer. The turmoil and confusion of that time complicated his thoughts. He finally said, "No. I really did want to come home to take care of my family. I hadn't planned to re-up for another tour. After the inquiry, I didn't have the heart for another go-round anyway."

He glanced over at Sadie, surprised to find her eyes had widened as she stared at him. But her expression quickly melted into a compassion he hadn't even known he was hoping for.

"Your family needs you," she said, then waved her hand through the air. "You need this. There's nothing wrong with it."

Taking the few short steps around the table, Zach knelt next to Sadie's chair and buried his face in her lap. His eyes were squeezed tight. He stayed there for a few minutes, taking comfort from her wisdom and willingness to share.

His grip tightened for a moment, unwilling to let go, and for the first time in over five years, he started to believe.

* * *

Sadie knew what she had to do the minute she got back to Black Hills, but still put it off for a few days. Every phone call from her mom increased her procrastination instead of spurring her to finish this farce. Every angry email, text and phone call from Victor increased her guilt.

The excuses were growing slim.

It hadn't helped that she'd been completely out of contact for four days. Rather than risk a call while she was with Zach, she'd simply shut her phone down, turning it on only to call her mother each night. She'd sent her pictures of the gorgeous scenery covered in snow, including some she took when they went hiking in the dense woods.

Those four days seemed like a space and time outside harsh reality. Now she had glorious memories of Zach to hold on to for years to come—years that were sure to be even lonelier and colder than the last five.

But she had to check one more thing about Zach. This was the last avenue open to her. If nothing came of it, she'd already determined that she wasn't going to lie just for the money. No matter how scared that left her.

She would call the lawyer, bypassing Victor completely, and tell him she would give an affidavit testifying to what Victor had hired her to do, all the avenues she'd explored and that Zach was squeaky-clean and eligible for his father's inheritance.

Then she'd walk away once more. At least if she disappeared she wouldn't have to see Zach's face when he realized who she really was, why she was really here.

It was the coward's way out—but her reserves of strength were leaking out with the speed of an hourglass. So she was looking into the only option left: Zach's military service.

The chance that she might have to use something so personal—his very intimate confession—against him...

Well, the thought made her sick to her stomach.

She'd done a preliminary search on her laptop, just to see if there was anything out there. Gaining access to military records wasn't an option, but if the incident was big enough, it might have been reported by local media outlets in the US, especially in the deceased's hometown.

Quite a few hits had shown up, but she didn't dare read them when Zachary could walk in at any moment. Lately he spent more time with her at the B and B than he did at home—though he never offered to take her to his place.

They spent so much time together, the landlady had casually mentioned charging her for a second person. Sadie had adopted a deadpan expression and said, "Sure"—which had left Gladys a little startled.

Now Sadie glanced around the local library, wondering exactly how to use the computer system. She figured doing this anonymously on a public computer was the safest way to go. If she signed in as a guest, no one would be able to trace it back to her.

Finding the bank of computers near the back of the building, she was grateful to see they were mostly unoccupied. She signed in at the desk, using her sister's name on the form. Then she chose the last computer on the end of the row, figuring there would be less chance of people reading over her shoulder.

Logging on, she retraced her internet search on this computer in a safe browser. Odds were, it was a useless precaution. After all, who would think to look at her browser history here? But just in case…

The first link happened to be to the website for the local Black Hills paper. Following it brought her to the electronic archives for the paper, but it needed a log-in for access. Deciding to come back to that, she tried a few more links.

The local paper for a small town in Pennsylvania wasn't password protected. Sadie was able to learn the name of Zach's friend who died, read the basics of his death and see pictures of him, his fellow soldiers and his grief-stricken family.

Sad. Very sad.

As if that wasn't heartbreaking enough, there were excerpts from Zach's speech at his friend's memorial service, held after the soldiers made their final trip home. But it was a random sentence, late in the article, that told her she had to search further. As commanding officer, Zach had faced an inquiry into his friend's death. No results were mentioned there, or in any other articles she read.

Frustrated, Sadie dropped back against her chair with a short sigh. What should she do now?

"Are you finding everything you need, ma'am?"

No. Sadie looked up into the face of a young woman who had a library volunteer tag on her shirt. No one had bothered her here in the corner, and Sadie had been grateful for the privacy. But maybe this young woman would know...

"Does the library have access to the local newspaper's archives?"

The woman smiled. "We have the oldest editions on microfiche, but we have a subscription to the modern edition that's available online."

Well, wasn't that handy. Sadie might have been happy if this wasn't such an awful thing to be doing.

The young lady got her logged in and showed her how to search the archives.

"So I can just put in a date range, like this?" Sadie asked, typing in the dates for the two months after the incident.

"Yes," the volunteer answered. "When you do that, it comes up in this neat preview version." The screen filled with rows of little preview boxes, each with a thumbnail picture inside and a date directly below it.

"Cool," Sadie said, scanning the pictures.

"You're the photographer lady, right?"

Startled, Sadie looked up at the girl. Cautiously,

she nodded, but the other woman didn't seem to notice her sudden reticence. What if she started blabbing about Sadie's search?

"I thought so," the young woman went on. "I saw you at the mill one day when I was there to take my dad some medicine while he was working on the cleanup. I heard some of the workmen talking about you." She reached across to take control of the mouse so she could choose one selection pretty close to the middle. "You might find this interesting, since I heard you were spending a lot of time with Zach Gatlin."

Sure enough, the preview had a photo of half of Zach's face on one side, something that Sadie hadn't had time to scan down to see yet. When the woman clicked, the front page of the paper loaded, including a story with the headline Hometown Hero Returns After Tragic Ending to Tour.

Sadie sat frozen, unwilling to believe the woman had picked out the very story she needed to read.

"It was the talk of the town, even before he came home," she went on. "He was lucky to even be alive. I just happened to be in Lola's when KC brought him home from the airport. I'll never forget his mama's face."

Having met Zach's mom and seen how much she loved her son, Sadie could very much imagine.

The young lady looked up as another employee appeared on the other side of the computer terminals and said, "Sweetie, Miss Jane needs a bit of a hand with story time, if you don't mind."

"Sure," the volunteer said with an eager smile, then turned to Sadie. "Hope that helps. If you need anything else, just flag one of us down." Sadie was grateful for her eagerness to help, but she needed to be alone...now.

"Will do." But Sadie sincerely hoped this was her last avenue of investigation.

It wasn't until the women walked away that Sadie read through the story. It looked as though Zach's involvement had indeed been questioned. But right below the picture of him and his sister embracing at the airport, it stated that he'd been found not guilty of any wrongdoing.

Sadie searched through nearly a month's worth of articles until she finally found the most in-depth account she could have gotten. It was obvious from the cautious tone of the article that the author didn't yet know the outcome of the inquiry.

According to the author's source, there were accusations of inadequate planning and reconnaissance, which could have meant anything, since the military was unlikely to release every detail that was being questioned. Zach was being held responsible in his friend's death, since he was the highest-ranking member of the team and had given the orders during the mission.

After reading all the way through, then one more time for good measure, Sadie cleared her browser history and closed the window. She leaned back, then looked up at the ceiling, as if the answer to her question could be found there. Even without her bias toward Zach, Sadie could tell this was just an instance of wrong place, wrong time. Zach had gotten off without even a reprimand, as far as she could tell.

But that didn't stop him from searching for what he could have done differently to save his friend. The nightmares were his mind's way of playing out his questions and his guilt. They were lessening with time, but would probably never go away.

That was punishment enough.

Now Sadie knew the truth. Her own search was over—her own guilt just beginning.

Fourteen

Sadie was once more wearing her fancy blue dress from the Blackstones' party, hoping those who had seen it before would understand she was from out of town and hadn't traveled with a steamer trunk full of formal gowns.

Her heart pounded as she waited for Zach, nausea welling up inside her. He'd paused to talk with the country club valet, whom he knew from working at the mill. If she could just stand here and watch him forever, she'd be so happy.

But deep down, she knew she had to end this to-night. Somehow she would find the courage to tell him the truth. He deserved to know how to claim his inheritance, and she'd decided he should hear it from her.

But first, just one more night together. One last memory.

Finally he headed her way, his dark good looks set off by the black suit and tie. She savored the way his gaze traced her body. No other man would make her feel as wanted as Zach did. She knew that beyond a doubt.

They joined the Blackstones at their table. Sadie realized she must be getting used to attending these events with Zach, because that feeling of unreality she usually experienced had disappeared. Too bad this wouldn't last. As soon as she returned to Dallas, she'd be extra busy looking for a new position. Hopefully in the same social circles her former boss had enjoyed, so she could continue to keep their heads above water as best she could.

Victor had continued to pay her regular salary, in addition to all of her travel expenses, as if she were on a regular business trip, instead of seeking to ruin a man's reputation. But when she came back empty-handed, all of that income would end.

She had some contacts within those social circles, so that might help. But her foremost concern was that her sister needed to remain close to the hospital and doctors who currently treated her. Sadie would hate to be separated from her family, but without the bonus from Victor, for finding dirt to disqualify

Zach from his inheritance, finding work would be essential.

Wherever she could find it.

Christina sat opposite Sadie. The tired cast to her face prompted Sadie's concern. The poor thing must be exhausted after handling her mother-in-law's death, plus her own grief and her pregnancy, too. "How are you, Christina?" Sadie asked quietly, not wanting to draw undue attention.

The other woman's smile seemed bittersweet. "I'm managing. Just trying to focus on what's right in front of us, you know?"

Sadie didn't, but she could imagine, so she nodded.

Before she could respond further, Aiden rose from his chair to look over the table. Everyone's attention turned to him. He appeared comfortable in his role as head of the family. His normally tough gaze as he took in those around him seemed to soften and glow. "Thank you for being here tonight. We wanted our family and closest friends here to celebrate the joy that is coming to our family—our newest baby, who will be joining us soon, along with the return of our brother Luke and his engagement to one of Black Hills's own treasures, Avery Prescott."

Quiet applause and smiles erupted. Sadie glanced down the length of the table, noting the people she recognized. Luke Blackstone and his fiancée were new to her, along with an older couple someone had mentioned were a doctor and his wife, friends of both the Blackstones and Prescotts, and mentors of Avery Prescott. Zach and Bateman and his family were there from the mill. She was impressed to see both Nolen and Marie present, along with a younger woman Marie had introduced to Sadie as her niece, Nicole. There was a mix of ages, stations in life and connections, but Sadie had found that the Blackstones embraced others based on their presence in their lives, not what they were capable of doing for them.

The viewpoint was refreshing for Sadie. She only hoped she could find future employers who were as real as the people she'd come to know here.

As they were served their meals, Sadie felt Zach's hand circle around her own. She turned to find him watching her with the fire and need she so desperately wanted to see in his eyes.

"You look beautiful tonight, Sadie," he said. "I love you in this dress."

Her throat closed for a moment. Hearing those first three words on his lips meant the world to her, even if he didn't mean them the way she wished. "I love you in that suit," she finally whispered. "Very dashing."

"Dashing, huh? Debonair, too?"

Oh, that grin was dangerous. "Most definitely."

"Well, I promise to be a gentleman." He leaned forward to brush a kiss high on her cheekbone, right in front of her ear. Then he whispered, "For now."

The shiver that worked its way down her spine

caused her to squeeze the hand still holding hers. How much longer could she hold him to her?

They were interrupted by the arrival of their food. Sadie leaned back as her soup was placed before her, followed by a plate of oysters for their end of the table to share. As she glanced over the half shells coated in some kind of breading and cheese mixture, her stomach turned over again.

She sucked in a breath through pursed lips, then slowly released it. *Nope, not helping.* "Excuse me a moment," she murmured to Zach.

Luckily she'd seen where the restroom was on their way inside. Her stomach had calmed again before she reached the door, but she went inside anyway. Running cool water over her wrists helped also. Lord, she needed to get her nerves under control. Life was never easy, but why ruin her last night with Zach by anticipating the earthquake that she knew was coming?

Did she even believe what she was telling herself right now?

The door opened behind her. Christina and KC stepped inside. Both women flocked to her with concern in their expressions.

"Are you okay?" Christina asked, patting her back gently.

She nodded as KC asked the same. "Yes, I've just been feeling a little off somehow."

"Zach was worried when you left so quickly. I

told him we would check, though you were probably fine."

"Sorry. Didn't mean to scare anyone."

"Well, I only have to make about fifty trips a
night to the bathroom right now," Christina said with
a laugh as she headed for a stall. "So I'd be here
soon enough anyway. If it had been any earlier in
my pregnancy, those oysters would have turned me
green. I wouldn't have even made it back here." She
flashed a grossed-out face over her shoulder before
shutting the door.

"Oh, me, too," KC said from beside Sadie as she
patted over her hair. "Of course, any kind of sea-
food got to me. It wasn't so much the look of it as the
smell. Yuck." She grinned. "I was so glad when that
stage went away, because I love me some shrimp."

Sadie felt her stomach twist again as her mind
conjured up the image of shrimp scampi, usually
one of her favorites. She breathed carefully, glancing at the mirror to make sure her queasiness didn't
show on her face. No need to cause more concern.

KC opened her little clutch purse and proceeded
to touch up her already perfect makeup. Christina returned and washed her hands. "It's not completely gone for me," she was saying. "The nausea
isn't nearly as bad as it was in the first trimester, of
course, but some things will still set it off sometimes.
And the exhaustion. Oh, boy."

"I know what you mean," KC agreed. "You have
more than just the pregnancy to make you tired, but

I sure remember trying to wait tables with swollen feet and that bone-tired feeling weighing me down. That was rough."

As the women talked around her, Sadie stared into the mirror. She could actually see the blood drain from her already pale skin. Her light dusting of freckles stood out in stark contrast, as did the glossy pink of her lips. Nausea. She'd put it down to nerves. Exhaustion. She'd simply pushed it aside as too many late nights with Zach.

Her gaze dropped to her chest, as she suddenly remembered the recent tenderness of her breasts. She'd chalked it up to hormones, but this would be about the third week they'd been unusually sensitive.

That wasn't normal.

"Are you coming, Sadie?"

She glanced up, realizing the others were readying to leave. "Oh, I'll just, you know." She nodded toward the stalls. "Then I'll be right out."

They smiled, sure they'd done their duty, then headed back out to their dinner. Sadie couldn't have felt less like eating.

As the sound of their chatter faded, she closed herself in a stall, leaning heavily against the inside of the door. Her mind raced, frantically counting out the days she'd been in Black Hills, the number of days since she'd first seen Zach again. Finally, the number of days since they'd made love that first time.

Please. Could she please just stop thinking? Stop remembering? But it was no use. She didn't have experience with pregnancy herself and had never been around anyone who was having a baby. Her time with Christina was as close as she'd gotten.

Which wasn't much. But based on how off she'd felt the last few weeks—something she'd chalked up to guilt, nerves and grief—Sadie was afraid she'd added one very large complication to her already tangled situation.

Heaven help her.

Zach lengthened his stride, hoping to make it through the foyer before Gladys heard the door close behind him. He didn't have long before he had to be at the office. KC was helping him get their newest team member settled in town. They were signing the paperwork on his new apartment before she brought him by the office for the first time.

Zach needed to be there.

But he was worried about Sadie. She'd gone home early from the dinner the night before, afraid she'd come down with a stomach bug. She'd even insisted on taking a cab home, expressing concern about interrupting the event and also about infecting him.

He'd let her go, only after she'd promised to text when she got back to the B and B. There were still things they didn't know about each other—for all he knew, she was the type who wanted to be left alone when she was sick. Like him.

She'd texted him when she got back and had even mentioned that she'd stopped at the pharmacy for some meds to help calm her stomach. He hadn't heard from her since.

A quick peek to assure himself that she was okay would be enough for now.

But later, they needed to have a talk. Zach was perfectly happy to let her be, as long as she touched base every so often to let him know she was okay. Preferably from the other end of the room, rather than the other end of town.

Otherwise, those dang protective instincts kicked in, and he worried something had happened—

Zach paused outside Sadie's door, hand raised to knock. The contrast between what he wanted with Sadie and what he had with her hit him hard. He'd proceeded on tiptoes, not demanding too much too soon, not asking for what he truly needed, afraid that if he pushed too hard, she would leave again.

Maybe he'd been overcautious. They were practically living together, and yet he'd let her go home sick without him the night before. He stood outside her door right now, waiting to knock, because he didn't want to intrude. How ridiculously careful all of this was.

With a frown, Zach tried the doorknob. It clicked, then opened. He walked inside. It was that easy.

Glancing around, he was alarmed to see the bed empty, blankets half hanging off the side, as if they had trailed after the person trying to leave them behind. No Sadie in sight. He heard the shower running.

Okay. She was steady enough to want to shower.

Good deal. He'd just wait until she got out. After making sure she didn't need anything, he'd head over to the office for a while, then come back. He crossed to the bed to straighten up the covers. A tissue box and mound of crumpled, used tissues covered the nightstand.

Odd, she'd said her stomach hurt, not that she had a cold.

Once more he looked around, this time hunting for the small trash can he knew to be around here somewhere. He finally located it under the low table in the sitting area. It was already filled with tissues. That explained one thing, at least. As he stood there wondering if he should risk calling Gladys for a new trash bag, Sadie's phone lit up.

An incoming text message.

He didn't recognize the name Victor Bedding-field, but the preview of the message on the screen below the name made Zach do a double take.

Hell no, I don't care what happens to Zach Gatlin, as long as he doesn't show up here wanting...

Wanting what? And why was this stranger texting about him?

The mere use of his name gave Zach the right to pick up that phone, in his opinion. And right now, his was the only opinion that mattered. He swiped his thumb over the screen. Zach only wished he could honestly say he didn't know Sadie's combination to unlock the screen. Unfortunately, it was a connect-the-dots picture that he'd watched her swipe in many times. The order of the combination played out in his mind's eye with ease.

He didn't even hesitate.

As a soldier, Zach knew that doing ugly things was sometimes necessary to get the job done. Right now, breaking into Sadie's phone was one of those necessary things. Regardless of how other people would see it.

A violation of her privacy? Sure. Overstepping his boundaries? Definitely. A decision he'd regret in time? Absolutely not.

Zach would rather know the truth than live in a fantasy world. The phone blinked its notice that Sadie had a text message at the bottom. He clicked on it and saw the truth in full color.

At the top of the screen, there was a text from Sadie in a white bubble: I will call soon.

Then a blue bubble from Beddingfield: If you don't call me within the hour, this is gonna get really ugly. I want this over. Do you hear me?

Followed by Sadie's response: Don't you care at all what happens to Zach? I'm trying very hard to do the right thing.

Hell no, I don't care what happens to Zach Gatlin, as long as he doesn't show up here wanting our father's money. You said you would dig up the dirt and I want it now. If you have to lie to disqualify him, that's what you'll do. I make the rules here. You simply obey me.

Deep in Zach's chest, coldness bloomed, then spread. Questions whirled in his brain. First and foremost: Who was this person? And what did he mean by "our father"? Was Victor Sadie's brother, talking about the two of them when he said "our"? But they had different last names.

Or was he Zach's brother?

Zach didn't know his father, so half or stepbrothers were definitely a possibility. Though the fact that his father would want to have other children when he couldn't be bothered to care for the one he already had was hard to take.

The second line of thought was the more painful one. He didn't even want to think about it. Didn't want to form the words that would rip apart the foundation he'd thought he was standing on for the last two months. But as the water shut off in the bathroom, he knew the detonation was coming.

The phone was still in his hand. He didn't bother to put it down, didn't bother to move. By the time Sadie came through the door, he'd even stopped breathing. That cold, cold part of him wanted to thaw, wanted to go to her.

Her long auburn hair was piled in a messy bun atop her head. She looked tired, her features slightly drawn. Her naked body was wrapped in one of the fluffy towels he'd often used to dry her. When she saw him, her eyes widened, but then she produced a small smile.

"Zach, you startled me," she said. "I didn't know you were coming."

Before he could speak, the phone in his hand rang. Her gaze flicked down to it, alarm invading her expression when she saw it in his hand. It played through an entire ringtone, then went silent. Zach's fingers tightened. Almost immediately the ringing started again.

Zach reached out, offering the phone to her. "Beddingfield wants an answer to his question," he said. "Don't you think you should take his call?"

Fifteen

The fact that she could take the phone from Zach's hand and switch it to mute actually amazed Sadie. Her body shook so hard she wouldn't have thought the move was even possible.

But she did it. Because she had to—because she deserved whatever Zach was about to dish out.

But she'd rather not do it in just a towel.

Turning away, she dropped the phone on the bed and reached for her robe. She hadn't even gotten it over her shoulders before Zach's questions started. She was actually surprised he'd waited at all.

"Who is Victor Beddingfield? Your brother? Your lover? Your what? Employer?"

Sadie's stomach turned, this time from more than

just the pregnancy she'd confirmed after a stop at the drugstore last night. She couldn't think of that now. Luckily, she hadn't eaten, so there wasn't anything to come up.

"Tell me now, Sadie."

She absorbed the blow of the staccato words as she tied the robe's belt around her waist. Then she faced Zach, attempting to keep her expression blank.

"Victor is my current—temporary—employer."

As if her calm answer infuriated him, Zach spoke next through gritted teeth. "And what the hell does he have to do with me?"

She slowly drew in a breath before answering. "He's your half brother."

Should she say more? This was one reason why she'd put off this moment—there were no guidelines telling her how much or how little information she should give to the man that she'd lied to for two months...no, five years.

"That doesn't tell me what he wants with me." Zach's harsh expression didn't give her any clues or guidance as to how to proceed.

Okay, here goes... "Your father recently passed away." She paused to give him a moment to absorb that, but his expression only grew harder. "There is a rather, um, large inheritance."

"Then this Beddingfield should take it and leave me alone. My father never wanted anything to do with me. Why would I want his money now?"

That wasn't technically true, but Sadie wasn't

going to explain that his father had sent her before. At least, not now.

"It isn't that easy," she said instead. "Victor can't inherit your father's estate because it has been willed to you."

Zach frowned, but didn't say anything.

"On one condition."

Then his gaze flipped to her phone on the bed before returning to her face. "The dirt?"

Reluctantly, she nodded. "You've been selected to receive the bulk of your father's estate, provided you haven't been immoral or corrupt in any way. There can be no arrests, convictions, scandals or incidents showing distinct lack of character in your—" she had to swallow "—history. Your father wanted to reward you for being a better man than he was."

"That's ridiculous."

Sadie shrugged. "Mr. Beddingfield played by his own set of rules."

"So you're, what, here to spy on me?"

Leave it to Zach to get to the heart of the matter.

"Wait. Were you here to spy on me before, too?"

Straight to the heart. "Yes." Why prevaricate? He was going to hate her anyway. She might as well cut the ties cleanly, even if the frost encasing her heart was starting to bite. "Your father sent me the first time." She could go into details later, if necessary. "Victor sent me this time—"

"To find out the truth? Or to make up some plausible lies?"

"Victor doesn't really care either way."

"He made that clear."

"But I can assure you, I'll be telling your father's lawyer the truth."

She couldn't stop herself from flinching as Zach stalked to her. He seemed to grow larger and more menacing as rage lit his features. "You know nothing about the truth. You've lied to me from the beginning, haven't you?"

"Not about the things that matter."

Rage mutated into disgust. "I doubt you have any idea what matters to me. None at all."

Oh, but she did. He valued family, loyalty, honesty, compassion, helping hands and going the extra mile. He was everything Victor wasn't. With each thing she'd learned about Zach, Sadie had known she fought a losing battle for his heart.

Because the core of her mission was the opposite of everything he held dear.

Only she couldn't turn away from these few weeks of pure bliss. That had been selfish on her part—indecisive, too. But she couldn't change it—not her choices, nor what had pushed her into those choices.

But she wasn't making excuses or asking forgiveness. She didn't deserve it.

"I'm sorry, Zach." It was as far as she could let herself go. Anything more and she'd fall to her knees right here, begging for the one thing he would never give her now: his love.

She expected him to let loose that rage on her.

To rant or throw things or scream. His father would have. His half brother certainly would have.

Zach did none of that.

Instead he turned and stalked to the door. He was probably done with her. But despite her resolutions, she found she couldn't keep one thing inside. The one thing he deserved to know.

"But I do have one last thing to say, Zach. And I mean it with everything in me. That you are a good man."

He paused before the door but didn't turn around, didn't grant her one last glimpse of a face carved in stone. Instead he said, "Pardon me if that offers very little consolation."

She was sure it didn't.

Somehow, some way, Zach managed to get through what he absolutely had to that afternoon without exploding, and then he ditched the rest of his appointments. His car ate up the miles to the airport. His only thought was of running, fast and far, but where—he didn't know.

The cabin wasn't an option right now. The memories were too fresh, would be too painful. Only now did he regret taking Sadie there, because even a complete makeover would never erase her presence in what had once been his sanctuary.

Anger had him pressing on the gas that much harder. He was anxious for speed even though it wouldn't really help anything. That's when his phone dinged to signal an incoming text.

Sadie. He knew it before he even looked. His instinct was to hurl the phone out the window, but that would be giving in too easily, so he forced himself to pull over and read the text instead.

I've gone home. The room at the B&B is paid thru end of week. Left some of ur things on table and some important papers for you. I'm so sorry. S

Zach let his eyes slide closed. He didn't want to see the screen, didn't want to read about how sorry she was. If she'd been sorry, she never would have lied to him. Hell, she never would have come here. Why would she do something so incredibly dishonest?

No, he didn't want to know. Motive didn't matter, because he refused to feel sorry for someone who would go to so much trouble to integrate herself into his life, his bed, just to find out if he was a bad person.

And who was his dad to judge? That man had never done anything good in his entire life. He'd abandoned Zach's mother when he was little, simply vanished, never paying a lick of child support or sending so much as a single birthday present or Christmas gift. They'd been okay. They'd made it without the old SOB. But that seemed to make the terms of his will even more ironic.

There had to be more to the story than what Sadie had told him.

Some important papers for you.

Dammit. He spun the car into a U-turn and headed back into town. No matter what he told himself, he really did want to know what was going on.

He flashed a strained smile at Gladys when she glanced out at him from the dining area as he made his way through, but didn't speak. Neither did she. Did she realize Sadie was gone? Or had Sadie simply left without saying anything so Zach would have a chance to come by and collect his stuff without Gladys's interference? He didn't know what to think anymore.

He let himself into the room, noticing Sadie's absence at once. The low table no longer held her laptop, just a pile of odds and ends. Her robe wasn't thrown over the high back of the winged chair near the dresser. Her extra fluffy blanket no longer graced her side of the queen-size bed.

But her vanilla-caramel scent still lingered in the air. Tantalizing, but also a reminder of how deceptive that sweetness truly was.

Zach dropped onto the couch in front of his stuff. A T-shirt he'd left here. A toiletry bag with an extra toothbrush and deodorant and things for his overnight stays. His black leather belt. He wished now that there hadn't been so many nights, that she hadn't made it so easy.

Next to the pile was a manila envelope. Zach

stared for a long time before he made himself reach
out and open it. The quality of the fax wasn't the
best, but it was still readable. The time stamp along
the top showed she'd had this sent not long after their
talk this afternoon.

The letterhead was from a lawyer's office in Dallas. The text below explained that this lawyer was in
the process of executing Zach's father's last will and
testament. Based on his father's unusual requests,
adequate time had been given to search every avenue necessary. If Zach had any questions, he was
welcome to call them for explanations.

Should he wish to refuse his inheritance, there
were instructions on how to do that and what that
would mean for him in terms of future claims. The
exact sum wasn't mentioned, but Zach was guessing
it was significant for a lawyer to have been hired to
set up something this elaborate.

The lawyer seemed like a man who knew what he
was doing. Zach planned to reserve judgment until
he had experience with the guy himself.

The envelope also contained what looked like
legal papers that Zach would look over in more depth
later. There was a photograph of a man Zach assumed to be his father. It was blurred with age. But
Zach wasn't that interested in the picture; he'd put his
father out of his mind long ago. After all, his father
hadn't been willing to think about Zach or his mother
when he'd left them. Zach had been four at the time.

There was a professional bio. From what Zach

read, his father had hit oil when he'd traveled to Texas a couple of years after abandoning them. Of course, he hadn't looked back to the family he'd left behind. Zach's mother had worked her fingers to the bone to provide for him, and later KC. She'd deserved better than that.

As if she'd known he would be curious, Sadie had printed an article about his father's stroke and how it had affected his company. Apparently he was well-known in the Dallas area. Zach scanned it and moved on to the next piece. It was another photo, this one of a younger man with distinct features matching his father's. This one was labeled Victor Beddingfield.

Zach couldn't help it—he studied the picture for any resemblance to his half brother. There were a few. Zach certainly hoped he didn't share the petulant expression and self-indulgent softness that didn't sit well on an adult male.

All in all, the envelope contained straightforward information that Zach could take or leave. It all depended on his plans. He put the papers back. He could find out pretty much everything he needed to know about the players in this game at his office, now that he knew where to start.

This time, he wasn't about to hesitate to dig hard and deep.

Standing, he loaded his arms with everything that belonged to him. He had no intention of leaving anything of himself in this place. As he moved toward the door, he remembered another time, the first time, when he'd faced the same choice. He'd had the chance to exit and never look back, but the lure of Sadie had been too strong.

He glanced toward the bed. The same one that had tempted him that first night here. Memories of nights wrapped around Sadie under those covers made him ache with a mixture of desire, sadness and anger. He wasn't sure if he'd ever get over that. Maybe one day he would. Maybe one day he wouldn't think of her at all, and he could live the rest of his life without thinking her name or remembering her face.

Maybe one day.

As he turned toward the door, a glimpse of something that didn't belong flashed in his periphery. Something neglected on the floor between the antique nightstand and the bed. Zach should leave it. After all, the odds of it being his were slim.

Still, his feet carried him forward, and he cursed himself the entire way for caring that she might have left something of herself behind.

He shifted his load into one arm then bent low and patted around for whatever it was. Finally his fingers brushed against something hard. Long and rounded, it fit easily in his hand as he picked it up.

Zach glanced down as he stood, then totally wished he hadn't.

His mind flashed back to another day. One when he found his sister crying all alone at the bar, late at night after everyone had left. In her hand was an identical white plastic stick with a plastic cap on the end. There were two solid pink lines in the little window in the middle. He dropped onto the bed, and wondered if this day could get any worse.

Sixteen

Sadie quietly let herself into her apartment early the next morning, her body beyond tired. Sitting at the airport on standby was hellish on a good day. Yesterday had been almost unbearable.

She set down her luggage and made her way down the hall into the living area. Maybe she could catch a few winks before her mother woke up to get ready to go to the treatment center to see her sister. How in the world Sadie would explain to either of them what had happened was beyond her at the moment.

Zach hadn't been the only person she'd lied to. Despite their desperate need, Sadie had known her mother and sister would have never condoned her cooperation with Victor's diabolical plan to disqualify

Zach from his inheritance. So she'd told them the same story: that their former employer had gifted her with the trip of her dreams to explore her photography.

Now she had to find a way to tell them the truth.

As she came into the spacious room, she saw her mother sleeping on the overstuffed couch. Sadie frowned, worried for a moment that something had happened. Or maybe her mother had fallen asleep waiting for her to arrive. But a soft sound drew her gaze in the other direction, where she found her sister propped in the recliner Sadie kept angled toward the line of windows along the front of the room.

But her sister wasn't watching the early-morning sun as it lit up the rolling lawns of the Beddingfield estate. Instead her gaze met Sadie's. Tears stung Sadie's nose and eyes as her sister gifted her with a weak smile of welcome.

Quickly crossing the room, she bent over and carefully pulled Amber close. She still had an IV attached to keep her from dehydrating. But otherwise she was awake, and the staff must have thought her well enough to come home for a while.

Bending down, she met her sister's eyes, green like her own, and whispered, "When did you get here?"

Amber grinned, though she didn't lift her head from where it rested on the chair. "Just yesterday. We were gonna Skype you last night, but when you called to say you were coming home we decided to surprise you."

"Well, I definitely am."

Her sister's thin hair had been cropped close, leaving a pale auburn halo of curls that highlighted the too-prominent cheekbones in her pale face. Sadie brushed her fingers over the softness. "How are you, kiddo?"

"My white blood count is closer to normal, for now. Electrolytes are good. And I tolerated this latest round of treatments better than they expected, so I got to come home a few days early."

"That's great."

"She's getting stronger," their mother said. Sadie glanced over at her; she hadn't moved but had opened her eyes to watch her daughters. "The doctors are quite pleased."

"I bet."

Any improvement in Amber's condition was considered wonderful at this stage. Their goal now was to halt the deterioration from the disease and keep her as pain-free as possible, without the disorientation and fatigue that could come from the wrong drug combinations.

"I'm so glad you're home," Amber said, reaching out to squeeze Sadie's hand.

The chill from her sister's skin always startled Sadie. She reached up with her other hand, creating a little sandwich pocket in an effort to warm the cold fingers with her own. It never seemed to help, but Amber told her it felt good, so Sadie had formed the habit over time.

"And just why are you home?" her mother asked.

Her tone said she knew something was up. Not that Sadie was very good at hiding things. Or maybe she was too good, since she'd been able to deceive Zach for so long. "It was time," she said simply.

It was more than time to cut the ties. Maybe Zach seeing that text was for the best, even though her breaking heart didn't think so. If it had been up to her, she inevitably would have delayed. And then where would she be?

She pressed her sister's hand a little more tightly. "You rest a bit. I'll fix you some tea," she said.

"That would be good." But Amber didn't close her eyes. Instead she turned back to gaze out the window. She'd often told Sadie that she slept enough at the treatment center, pumped up on pain meds and other drugs. When she was home, she wanted to experience life, even if it was only through the window of their apartment.

Trying hard not to let a new wave of tears overwhelm her, Sadie retraced her steps down the hall to the kitchen. As expected, Sadie's mother joined her.

"For someone who has just been on the trip of their dreams, you do not look like you had a very restful time," her mother said quietly.

Sadie appreciated her mother's attempt to keep Amber from hearing her.

"That's because I lied," she said, figuring the straightforward approach was probably best.

There was no shock from her mother, only an understanding nod. "I see."

Why did life have to be so hard? "I did a very bad thing, Mom."

"I'm sure you did."

Sadie glanced over in surprise, spilling a bit of water over the edge of the electric kettle. "What? Why would you think that?"

"Sadie," she said with a sad shake of her head, "when was Mr. Beddingfield ever involved in anything good? Yes, he might have changed his perspective somewhat on his deathbed, but that man never did something only from goodness. There was always an ulterior motive."

Ulterior motive indeed. "Mr. Beddingfield didn't send me on this trip. Victor did."

Her mother's eyes widened. "Yes, I can see why you didn't share that with me. There is nothing benevolent in that man. I was surprised to even come home to find our stuff still here yesterday. I couldn't figure out why he hasn't made us leave the estate yet."

"It was part of our agreement," Sadie confessed.

Then she went on to tell her mother the how and why of her trip back to Black Hills, South Carolina. About halfway through she looked away, unable to bear what was sure to be her mother's disappointment in her. She managed to keep the tears at bay until she mentioned the baby she was now sure she carried.

The silence of several minutes was only broken by the release of steam from the kettle. Sadie couldn't bring herself to steep her sister's tea. Instead she remained with her arms braced against the counter, praying that the pain in her heart would ease enough to let her breathe again.

"So this man, Zach, will we be seeing him again?" her mother asked.

Sadie nodded. "I'll have to tell him about the baby, but it was so new, I just…couldn't." A deep breath braced her for her latest decision. "I will contact him soon enough, but I want to be established in a new job, a new place to live. I just couldn't bear to give him the impression that I told him about the baby to get some of his money."

"But Sadie, how will we afford—"

"I don't know. We just will. Somehow." But she knew beyond a doubt she couldn't face asking Zach for money. She wasn't even sure she would be able to take it if he offered. So much of this whole situation had been motivated by her struggles to simply keep their heads above water.

But other people would only see it as greed.

"We will figure something out," she assured her mother with a false smile. "I'll start looking for another job today. One thing—the only good thing—Mr. Beddingfield did was to safeguard me against any attempt Victor made to discredit me. I have a certified reference from him, with his lawyer's signature as witness. That will at least give me a place to start."

Some of the strain on her mother's face eased. "Yes, it will help. I could look for something—"

"Absolutely not." They'd had this discussion time and again. "Amber needs you with her. We both know that. I'll fix this, somehow."

Even if the solution was a complete and total mystery to her right now.

Zach took a seat in the substantial waiting area at the offices of Beddingfield's lawyer, Timberlake. Apparently, Beddingfield Senior had been a big man in town, and he'd paid for the best in everything. Including lawyers.

Zach couldn't bring himself to think of the man as his father. He'd contributed DNA, but that was about it.

Except now, after his death, he was about to gift Zach with a fortune that still boggled his mind, according to his phone conversations with the lawyer. Beddingfield hadn't just hit it big in the oil business after coming to Texas, he'd then diversified, which had protected his assets from market fluctuations and downturns. Zach would be in a tax bracket far removed from the one he'd moved into after opening his own business. The thought was so far outside reality that he'd stopped trying to comprehend it.

But in terms of the man who'd sired him—it was a case of too little, too late.

Zach had chosen to make an impromptu trip to Dallas before telling his family all that had transpired. He preferred to have all the facts at hand first.

Besides, his sister had become increasingly curious about Sadie, not buying Zach's excuse that she'd returned home for a family emergency. Of course, after his investigation into her history, that excuse might not have been as far from reality as he'd thought when he made it up.

Sadie had told the truth about some things. This time around, Zach hadn't held back, using all the resources at his disposal when it came to investigating her. She'd used her real name. According to her tax records, she'd indeed been an employee of Beddingfield Senior for several years. And her mother had held the same position for the same employer until the year Sadie took over. Her mother had no employment records since then.

The few things Zach had been able to find out about Sadie's younger sister's illness had confirmed what he knew: she'd been ill a very long time and her prognosis was terminal.

The most eye-opening portion of his investigation had been his inquiries into Sadie's finances. That's when he'd started to feel dirty. She didn't have the usual expenses of a woman her age. No apartment or housing loan. No car loan, either. Two maxed-out credit cards that hadn't had any activity recorded in two years, other than payments. And astronomical debts to several medical institutions in the Dallas area.

Sadie was apparently financially responsible for all of her sister's medical bills.

As much as Zach didn't condone lying and dishonesty, factoring Beddingfield's huge fortune into Sadie's crippling financial situation didn't add up to a woman spying on him on a whim. He wanted more information before he confronted her about the little bombshell he'd discovered at the B and B after she left.

Feeling restless, as thoughts about Sadie often made him, Zach stood up. He prowled around the empty area for several minutes before coming to a stop in front of a long bank of windows overlooking busy traffic on the streets below. Coming to the office at the end of the day, he'd known he would wait for an extended period of time. Probably until after Timberlake's last client left.

But he'd see Zach—the man about to take the place of his, and his firm's, biggest client.

Zach heard a rumble down the hallway, the sound of a raised voice behind a closed door. He glanced over at the receptionist, who looked uneasily toward the glass wall behind her. When she noticed him watching, she flashed a strained smile and pretended to get back to work.

The rumble increased, and Zach realized other voices had joined the fray. One of the lawyers must have a very unhappy client. Just as a door in the back hallway opened, the receptionist's phone rang. She answered with a clipped, "Yes, sir." Then she immediately hung up and redialed. "We need assistance on floor four near the conference room, please," she said in a slightly raised voice.

The commotion in the hallway got louder. Zach wasn't sure what was happening but decided to offer his assistance regardless until security could arrive. Just as he reached the receptionist's desk, a man's voice rang out.

"I will get you for this. You will never work in this city again, you hear me! Not only will you not see a dime from me, but I'll see to it that you'll never find a way to support that dying brat, either."

The sound of men's voices protesting and the shuffling of dress shoes carried through to the reception area. One was louder than the rest. "Mr. Beddingfield, stop right now. There's nothing to be gained by this behavior."

"There's nothing to be gained by me being a Goody Two-shoes, either. This bitch just cut me off from my inheritance. She's gonna pay."

The elevator dinged as the doors opened, heralding the arrival of two security guards. But the raucous group in the hallway now appeared around the corner, plainly visible through the glass wall behind the receptionist.

Zach saw Sadie jump backward just as a male hand grabbed for her. A sharp cry rang out. The men around her dropped their polite facades. Yelling commenced as they tried to force Victor Beddingfield back. The security guards waded into the fray, quickly subduing the man Zach now knew was his half brother. He watched as they cuffed the tall man, whose blond good looks made him Zach's polar opposite.

As did his spoiled attitude.

A stocky, gray-haired man guided Sadie back with an arm around her shoulders. For the first time in a month he glimpsed her wealth of auburn hair and full features through the wavy glass. He couldn't make out her expression with precision, except to tell that her lips were pulled into a frown. By the time he looked back at Victor, the security guards were leading him back down the hallway.

A few low words were exchanged with the other two gentlemen, then one broke away and followed the guards. After a few minutes, the gray-haired man led Sadie around the opposite side of the glass wall and over to the elevator bank.

They never even glanced in Zach's direction.

"Thank you again, Ms. Adams, for coming in to give your deposition. I'm very, very sorry for the commotion. I have no idea how Mr. Beddingfield found out you would be here today."

Sadie shook her head, but Zach could see that her hand remained clasped over the front of her throat. Her arms were pressed close against her torso. "No, it's not your fault. I just hope I've done what I can to make sure y'all know the truth about Zachary Gatlin."

An electric pulse set Zach on edge as he heard his name on her lips. He knew it shouldn't affect him—or rather, he shouldn't let it affect him. But he was a man who'd been in love, after all.

He stood quietly as the two finished their conversation. The lawyer, whom Zach now knew to be Timberlake, delivered her carefully into the elevator, as if worried about any lasting effects from the confrontation. Only as she faced the reception area once more did she glance beyond where the lawyer stood.

Her eyes widened in surprise just as the doors slid closed.

Seventeen

"Will she?"

"Pardon me?" The lawyer's confused look confirmed Zach had spoken out loud, even though he hadn't intended to.

"Will Sadie be able to support her sister? Or will Beddingfield be able to keep her from getting work?"

The confusion cleared. "Oh, no. He won't be able to poison future employers against her—I drafted your father's reference letter for Ms. Adams myself. Plus, she has a good reputation with the people who have visited his home over the years. She'll be fine, professionally."

Zach sensed something more. "But?"

"I'm afraid I don't know of a job in her field that will pay enough to take care of the medical bills."

Zach knew about that all too well.

Timberlake leaned forward, his expression earnest. After their conversations over the phone, Zach had found him to be someone he felt pretty comfortable with. The man's motives seemed straightforward.

"I wouldn't normally say this," he started, "but I know you've met Sadie personally. The deposition she gave is proof of that."

"Was it now?"

"The contents will be made public in court, but yes, she was very clear about your values, your family and the respect you have from your business associates. She explained in detail her efforts and inability to find any complaints against you or any criminal activity."

Zach hadn't realized that she would be so thorough in her report.

The lawyer went on. "I wonder if you know what a gift that is?"

Zach raised his brows in question.

"She didn't have to do that. She could easily have lied. If she had, she'd have been set for life."

What? "I don't understand."

"She confided to me, when she first came in, that Victor Beddingfield had offered her a quarter of the inheritance if she could find anything that would disqualify you. That money would have more than paid for her sister's treatments. Sadie would never have had to work again."

That was the truth. From everything he'd seen, a quarter of the inheritance, even after exorbitant estate taxes, would still be a fortune. A fortune Sadie desperately needed.

"But she never spoke against me?"

Timberlake shook his head. "Not a word." His gaze met Zach's directly. "Look, I'm not telling you this because I expect anything. I'm going to connect Sadie with some organizations that might be able to help her with her sister's treatments from here on out. But once you have that debt, it often can't be wiped away...at least not in any way that Sadie would accept."

The lawyer smiled sadly. "I could tell from the way she spoke that Sadie is not neutral in your case." He raised his hands. "I don't know what happened, and I don't care. But I think she should at least get credit for trying to do the right thing—in the end."

Could he do the same? Zach wasn't sure. He wanted to, and Lord knew he and Sadie had one more major hurdle to cross before their future was decided. He would never be able to leave the mother of his child behind completely. And he wasn't enough of an asshole to cut her out of their lives, even if that had been his first instinct.

Everyone made bad decisions when they were angry.

"There's something else," the lawyer said. The curiosity in his eyes making Zach just a little nervous.

"Yes?"

"Sadie has asked me to contact a family named Blackstone, and see that the pictures she took in

Black Hills were copyrighted to them to do with as they wish."

Holy hell.

"She also provided the name of a publisher who was interested in the story."

Why? Zach thought back to that pregnancy test and tried to imagine how she must have felt when she took it. She could have been elated…could have imagined all of her problems were fixed with the luck of the draw. After all, one DNA test and he would be legally liable for at least child support. With the inheritance he had coming, she could probably have jockeyed for a lot more than that. But if that were so, why would she have subjected herself to Beddingfield and having to give her deposition alone? Given up the rights to pictures that he knew meant more to her than the money?

One phone call to Zach could have put her on top of the world instead of the bottom rung. One call she'd refused to make to save herself from a lot of worry and fears.

But was this proof enough that he could trust her?

A quick change into clean clothes had helped Sadie feel more in control after her ugly experience with Victor at the lawyer's office. But she also felt an increased need to get them packed and out of the apartment over Mr. Beddingfield's renovated horse barn.

A need that rose exponentially after realizing Zach was now in town.

She could have gone back into the office, could have asked what he'd seen and heard and tried to defend herself against any ugly things Victor might tell him about her. But what was the point?

Zach already had enough ammunition to blast her out of his life. Anything more would just be overkill.

Still, she needed to get her family moved. The probate of the will would be moving forward, and hopefully one of the interviews she'd had over the last week would pan out for a new job. She'd found a medical halfway house that would let her mother and sister stay temporarily while Sadie arranged for a new place. All the apartments on the cheap end had been scary, but with her credit, something small in a bad neighborhood was the best she could do.

If her luck turned around, her new position would also offer living accommodations, or at least a supplement toward her rent. Fingers crossed on that one.

She moved down the hall to her sister's bedroom, stepping into the circle of cardboard boxes and packing tape and scissors she'd left there earlier. She'd splurged by hiring a mover, simply because her mother was completely unable to lift anything. Moving furniture alone wasn't an option, but Sadie wanted to pack all of the keepsakes and items with sentimental value herself.

The sun had completely disappeared by the time a knock sounded on the apartment door. She must have lost track of time, moving from her sister's bedroom to her own. The five full boxes now standing in the hallway attested to her progress.

The knock sounded again as she crossed the kitchen into the hallway. "I'm coming," she hollered, wondering if it was one of the staff from the big house.

Even though she wasn't technically employed anymore, they still showed up to ask her questions about various things. With that in mind, she flung the door open without thinking…and came face-to-face with Zachary Gatlin.

Panicked, she turned on her heel and strode back to the kitchen. Her quick steps took her all the way to the other side of the kitchen island. Only when she was facing the door with something solid between them did she feel a little more secure.

And slightly stupid for her reaction.

As he came through the door, words started to tumble out of her mouth. "Zach, I want to assure you we are in the process of moving. I've gotten everything arranged and we will be out—"

"Shush."

Sadie felt her eyes bug out a little at his harsh tone, though she wasn't sure why. It was nothing more than what she'd expected. "I just didn't want you to think—" she spotted his glare, but couldn't seem to stop "—we were…taking…advantage…now that you own the estate."

"Well, it's a little early in the process, but I will be looking into the estate and how it is run pretty soon." Zach spoke a little more mildly this time. "Still, I don't believe I said anything about you leaving."

"I just assumed…"

His raised brow told her exactly what he thought of that.

Maybe he was right. She should just shush. Everything she said right now was coming out wrong.

"Do you know why I'm here, Sadie?"

"Apparently it's not to throw me out of what is now your apartment."

He simply stared. "Sarcasm isn't pretty."

No, but it was her go-to option in this bizarre situation that she was completely unprepared for. Unless she chose honesty—and that was a scary thought. "No, Zach. I really don't know why you would want to see me."

He took a step closer to the island. "No reason at all?"

Sure—if he knew about the baby. But he didn't, and she wasn't ready to tell him yet. She would later, after everything was settled. "After what I did to you, Zach? No."

"The lawyer told me about your deposition."

Shock shot through her. That was the last thing on her mind. "Oh. I thought it would be kept private until the hearing."

Zach shrugged. "Does it really matter when I learn what's in it?"

"I guess not," she murmured, though she wished he hadn't learned about it while she was here. She could have done without a face-to-face discussion.

"And about the photos. Why, Sadie?"

Then his tone caught her attention.

She simply couldn't meet his gaze. "It's not right for me to keep them, not after…"

"You lied to me, Sadie."

"Yes, yes, I did," she said, dropping her gaze to the countertop. "I'm sorry, but I did lie to you." What more could she say?

"Why?"

This was exactly what she didn't want. She shook her head. "Zach, excuses won't change it."

"Try me."

She straightened her shoulders but still couldn't force herself to look at him. "The first time, I didn't know you."

"But then you did."

Why torture herself by admitting the truth? Why torture him? But with him standing so close, yet so far out of her reach, her need prodded her. He deserved the truth—the whole thing. "I did know you," she said, though her voice was so weak as to be almost nonexistent. "And it scared me so badly, all I knew to do was run."

"Five years, Sadie." The pure anguish in his voice twisted her heart. One look confirmed the same emotion in his expression. "Why didn't you come back to me?"

His cry echoed inside her, forcing her reality into words. "Why would a man like you want a woman with all my problems?" She grasped the edge of the counter until her knuckles turned white and her fingers went numb. "I'm sure the lawyer must have told you—the real me is nothing like that Sadie."

"She's not?" His voice softened. "Are you sure?"

"Yes." *Most definitely.*

He moved closer until he was flush with the other

side of the counter. They were as close as they could be in this space. "I'm not sure, Sadie. Because the woman I knew was compassionate and interested in people. Organized and hardworking. Artistic and able to see the beauty in the world, even in the midst of destruction."

Tears welled up, forcing her to squeeze her eyes closed.

"Isn't that the same as what you do here? Take on a hard job at a young age so your mother can stay home with your sister? Care about the people you meet in your job every day? Worry about your mother being tired, even though you're the one on your feet for twelve hours? Teach your sister to appreciate the world around her, even though she's dying? Sounds like the same Sadie to me."

She couldn't stop the tears. They dribbled down her cheeks without her permission.

"But she's also prideful."

Her lashes automatically lifted, her gaze connecting with his. "What?"

"Sadie only wants to be the caregiver, not the receiver."

So? "Doesn't everyone?"

"No." Zach's dark eyes offered compassion, but he didn't back down. "Lots of people want their dirty jobs done for them. They ignore the hard parts of life. You power through them."

"That's a problem?" she asked.

"Only when it makes you blind to other people's desire to help care for you." He leaned forward over the island between them. "It took me five long years to become vulnerable to you, Sadie. Don't you think I deserved the same?"

She took a step back, needing space, needing to breathe. "But me being vulnerable, opening up to you would have placed an obligation on you. A demand, even if it was unspoken, for you to take care of me and my problems."

"It's never an obligation when you love someone."

That took her breath away. "I've never had someone love me that way," she murmured.

"Haven't you?"

That dark gaze wouldn't let her look away, wouldn't let her pretend to not see the truth. "Yes."

Silence stood between them for long minutes, almost as if the world held its breath, waiting to see what came next. Sadie wasn't sure what it was.

Finally Zach spoke. "I want you to do something for me, okay?"

She nodded, not trusting herself to speak.

"When you're ready, truly ready, for me to love you that way…you let me know. Okay?"

A tremble started deep inside. What he asked seemed like almost too much.

"Okay?"

She could barely get the word out. "Yes."

"Goodbye, Sadie."

Her whole body screamed in protest, but she kept her lips sealed as he walked away. She could hear his footsteps down the hallway, then the click as he opened the door.

"Wait. Zach," she called, then forced her timid

feet to follow him. She paused a few feet away from where he waited by the front door. "I—I know I disappointed you." She swallowed at the lump trying to form in her throat. "But there's something you need to know. You can't leave without knowing… two things, actually."

He nodded, but didn't encourage her by word or any further gesture.

"One is… I love you. I'll always be glad that I experienced loving you, even though I screwed it up so badly."

His expression didn't change, and she died a little inside. But this had to be done.

"And two?" he asked.

She almost couldn't say it, almost told him to leave, but that was as selfish as every choice she'd made up until now. "Two is—I'm pregnant."

"I know."

"I don't want you to feel obligated—wait, what?"

Now she detected a touch of amusement in his voice. "I already know."

And from his softening expression, she knew he accepted it. "How?" she breathed.

Very gently, he closed the door. "You dropped the test. I found it when I went to get my things."

Sadie groaned, collapsing with her back to the wall. "Oh, goodness. I was putting it back in the box to bring home with me. I knew if I threw it away there—"

"Miss Gladys would have found it and the whole town would know, not just me?"

"Right." She opened her eyes to find him right in front of her. "I was trying to figure out how to tell you without making you feel…"

"Obligated?"

She nodded. "And I knew I couldn't do that with you looking at me, touching me. So I thought it was better to wait." She offered a halfhearted smile. "After what happened between KC and Jake, I couldn't keep your child from you. I wouldn't do that, Zach."

"I know that now."

"You do? How?"

"You just showed me. Thank you for trusting me with the truth, Sadie."

"So you aren't angry?"

He shook his head, stepping in until they stood body to body. "I'm not angry. We have a lot of things to work out, and I think we will both have to learn to let someone else take care of us, instead of always being the strong one." He brushed his lips gently over hers, leaving her weepy and boneless.

"We can make all of this work," he said, "but I think it's gonna take the two of us."

"You don't mind?"

"Never have."

That's when she started to weep in earnest. And Zach stood right there with her, supporting her through the storm.

"I love you, Sadie," he said when she finally quieted.

"Oh, Zach, I love you, too."

For long minutes neither of them spoke. They simply held each other and let their bodies confirm what they had known all along.

"Just promise me one thing," Sadie finally murmured.

"What's that?"

"That you will never do anything for me or my family that you don't feel completely comfortable doing," she insisted.

"The same here," he said.

After she nodded, he added, "And never walk away without letting me know where you're going."

"It's a deal."

* * * * *

*Pick up all the Harlequin Desire novels
from Dani Wade*

*HIS BY DESIGN
A BRIDE'S TANGLED VOWS
THE BLACKSTONE HEIR
THE RENEGADE RETURNS*

***

*If you're on Twitter, tell us what you think
of Harlequin Desire! #harlequindesire*

#2473 THE RANCHER RETURNS
The Westmoreland Legacy • by Brenda Jackson
When a Navy SEAL returns home, he finds a sexy professor digging
up his ranch in search of treasure! He wants her off his land...and in his
arms! But his family's secrets may stand in the way of seduction...

#2474 THE BLACK SHEEP'S SECRET CHILD
Billionaires and Babies • by Cat Schield
When his brother's widow comes to Trent Caldwell asking him to save
the family company, he knows exactly what he wants in return. First,
complete control of the business. Then the secretive single mother
back in his bed...

#2475 THE PREGNANCY PROPOSITION
Hawaiian Nights • by Andrea Laurence
When plain Paige flies to a Hawaiian resort to fulfill her grandfather's
dying wish, she's tempted by the hotel's handsome owner. Will her
unplanned pregnancy ruin their chance at giving in to more than desire?

#2476 HIS SECRET BABY BOMBSHELL
Dynasties: The Newports • by Jules Bennett
After their secret affair, Graham Newport discovers Eva Winchester is
pregnant! Her father is Graham's most hated business rival, but he's
ready to fight for Eve and their baby...as long as he can keep his heart
out of the negotiations!

#2477 CONVENIENT COWGIRL BRIDE
Red Dirt Royalty • by Silver James
Chase Barron needs a wife without pesky emotional expectations.
Down-on-her-luck cowgirl Savannah Wolfe needs help getting back
on the rodeo circuit. A marriage of convenience may solve both their
problems—unless they fall in love...

#2478 HIS ILLEGITIMATE HEIR
The Beaumont Heirs • by Sarah M. Anderson
Zeb Richards has never wanted anything more than he wants
the Beaumont's prized company. Until he meets top employee
Casey Johnson. Now this boss is breaking all the rules for just one
night—a night with consequences...

REQUEST YOUR FREE BOOKS!
2 FREE NOVELS PLUS 2 FREE GIFTS!

H HARLEQUIN®

Desire

ALWAYS POWERFUL, PASSIONATE AND PROVOCATIVE

YES! Please send me 2 FREE Harlequin® Desire novels and my 2 FREE gifts (gifts are worth about $10). After receiving them, if I don't wish to receive any more books, I can return the shipping statement marked "cancel." If I don't cancel, I will receive 6 brand-new novels every month and be billed just $4.55 per book in the U.S. or $5.24 per book in Canada. That's a savings of at least 13% off the cover price! It's quite a bargain! Shipping and handling is just 50¢ per book in the U.S. and 75¢ per book in Canada.* I understand that accepting the 2 free books and gifts places me under no obligation to buy anything. I can always return a shipment and cancel at any time. Even if I never buy another book, the two free books and gifts are mine to keep forever.

225/326 HDN GH2P

Name _____ (PLEASE PRINT)

Address _____ Apt. #

City _____ State/Prov. _____ Zip/Postal Code

Signature (if under 18, a parent or guardian must sign)

Mail to the **Reader Service:**
IN U.S.A.: P.O. Box 1867, Buffalo, NY 14240-1867
IN CANADA: P.O. Box 609, Fort Erie, Ontario L2A 5X3

**Want to try two free books from another line?
Call 1-800-873-8635 or visit www.ReaderService.com.**

* Terms and prices subject to change without notice. Prices do not include applicable taxes. Sales tax applicable in N.Y. Canadian residents will be charged applicable taxes. Offer not valid in Quebec. This offer is limited to one order per household. Not valid for current subscribers to Harlequin Desire books. All orders subject to credit approval. Credit or debit balances in a customer's account(s) may be offset by any other outstanding balance owed by or to the customer. Please allow 4 to 6 weeks for delivery. Offer available while quantities last.

Your Privacy—The Reader Service is committed to protecting your privacy. Our Privacy Policy is available online at www.ReaderService.com or upon request from the Reader Service.

We make a portion of our mailing list available to reputable third parties that offer products we believe may interest you. If you prefer that we not exchange your name with third parties, or if you wish to clarify or modify your communication preferences, please visit us at www.ReaderService.com/consumerschoice or write to us at Reader Service Preference Service, P.O. Box 9062, Buffalo, NY 14240-9062. Include your complete name and address.

HDI5

SPECIAL EXCERPT FROM

HARLEQUIN

Desire

Navy SEAL Gavin Blake has returned home to the ranch he loves to make sure beautiful Layla Harris leaves his family's spread...

Read on for a sneak peek at
THE RANCHER RETURNS,
by New York Times *bestselling author*
Brenda Jackson,
the first in **THE WESTMORELAND LEGACY** *series!*

Gavin grabbed his duffel from the truck. He tilted his Stetson back on his head and looked at the car parked in front of his grandmother's guest cottage. Gavin hoped his grandmother hadn't extended an invitation for that professor to stay on their property as well as dig on their land. He didn't want anyone taking advantage of his family.

He'd taken one step onto the porch when the front door swung open and his grandmother walked out. She was smiling, and when she opened her arms, he dropped his duffel bag and walked straight into the hug awaiting him.

"Welcome home, Gavin," she said. "I didn't expect you for a few months yet. Did everything go okay?"

He smiled. She always asked him the same thing, knowing full well that because of the classified nature of his job as a SEAL, he couldn't tell her anything. "Yes, Gramma Mel, everything went okay. I'm back because—"

He blinked, not sure he was seeing straight. A woman stood in the doorway, but she wasn't just *some* woman. She had to be the most gorgeous woman he'd ever seen. Hell, she looked like everything he'd ever fantasized a woman to be, even while fully clothed in jeans and a pullover sweater.

Gavin studied her features, trying to figure out what had him spellbound. Was it the caramel-colored skin, dark chocolate eyes, dimpled cheeks, button nose or well-defined, kissable lips? Maybe every single thing.

Not waiting for his grandmother to make introductions, his mouth eased into a smile. He reached out his hand and said, "Hello, I'm Gavin."

The moment their hands touched, a jolt of desire shot through his body. Nothing like this had ever happened to him before. From the expression that flashed in her eyes, he knew she felt it, as well.

"It's nice meeting you, Gavin," she said softly. "Layla Harris."

Harris? His aroused senses suddenly screeched to a stop. Did she say *Harris*? Was Layla related to this Professor Harris? Was she part of the excavation team?

Now he had even more questions, and he was determined to get some answers.

Don't miss
THE RANCHER RETURNS
by New York Times *bestselling author Brenda Jackson,*
available October 2016 wherever
Harlequin® Desire books and ebooks are sold.

www.Harlequin.com

Whatever You're Into... Passionate Reads

Looking for more passionate reads from Harlequin®?
Fear not! Harlequin® Presents, Harlequin® Desire and
Harlequin® Blaze offer you irresistible romance stories
featuring powerful heroes.

♦HARLEQUIN *Presents*

Do you want alpha males, decadent glamour and jet-set
lifestyles? Step into the sensational, sophisticated world of
Harlequin® Presents, where sinfully tempting heroes ignite a
fierce and wickedly irresistible passion!

♦HARLEQUIN *Desire*

Harlequin® Desire novels are powerful, passionate and
provocative contemporary romances set against a backdrop of
wealth, privilege and sweeping family saga. Alpha heroes with
a soft side meet strong-willed but vulnerable heroines amid a
dramatic world of divided loyalties, high-stakes conflict and
intense emotion.

♦HARLEQUIN *Blaze*

Harlequin® Blaze stories sizzle with strong heroines and
irresistible heroes playing the game of modern love and lust.
They're fun, sexy and always steamy.

Be sure to check out our full selection of books
within each series every month!

www.Harlequin.com

HPASSION2016